Dear Twin

Addie Tsai

Dear Twin

Addie Tsai

METONYMY PRESS
Montreal, Quebec

First edition
First printing - 2019
Printed in Canada by Marquis Book Printing
Pinyin editing by Alvis Choi
Cover and illustrations by Keet Geniza
Author photo by Cutloose Salon

Metonymy Press
PO Box 143 BP Saint Dominique
Montreal, QC H2S 3K6
Canada
metonymypress.com

Library and Archives Canada Cataloguing in Publication

Title: Dear twin / Addie Tsai.
Names: Tsai, Addie, 1979- author.
Identifiers: Canadiana (print) 20190167025 | Canadiana (ebook) 20190167297 | ISBN 9781999058807
 (softcover) | ISBN 9781999058821 (ebook)
Classification: LCC PS3620.S25 D43 2019 | DDC j813/.6—dc23

for those who are twinned
for those who are lost

There can be no friendship between twins: they are too close, so the only way for each of them to maintain his identity is to liquidate the other. A friend has to be outside my reach, beyond my grasp. And there can be no friendship with someone whom I am not ready to betray: a friend is someone I can betray with love. —Žižek

Contents

Do you think all twins want the other twin to die?

Either that, or they want to fold into each other,
to become one body.

Isn't that just another way of saying the same thing?

Prologue

I wanted her back. I knew it was a mission likely to fail. But I had to try.

It's been a month already since Lola's sudden, but not altogether unexpected, disappearance. No note, no return address, no calls, no texts. At first, we thought she was in one of her moods, or had run off with Sara or Kelcey doing god knows what. But they both insisted—Sara barely comprehensible through her tears, Kelcey out of breath, her words crashing into each other—that they hadn't seen her. At first, we tried calling. Baba sat for several days and nights glued to the chair next to the landline, pressing REDIAL again and again and again. Then he tried using his wife's phone. That was before. Before she couldn't take it anymore, and fled to Paris. He even tried borrowing his friends' phones while he was out—I only knew this because I overheard him whispering to my stepmother in Mandarin the night before she left, and caught what little I could: jiè, péngyǒu, diànhuà—thinking maybe if Lola didn't recognize the number as ours, she might answer. The day Mom learned Lola was gone, just like that, she sang her truest note: she left, too. Now that I think back, leaving had always been her go-to, so I should have known better. It still stung. Besides, I was still here. And Lola was still out there, somewhere. Anything could happen.

It was agony, but I waited until Baba exhausted himself and

I thought enough time had passed that she'd have settled down from whatever had made her leave. I tried emails, texts, phone calls. I tried imploring her with inside jokes told in the sweetest, most nonthreatening tone I could muster. I tried anger. Desperation. Despair. Begging. Weeping. I imagined her listening to the messages, hearing a voice made of the same range of decibels, the same lilting lisp as her own. Nothing worked.

As the Lola-shaped hole grew larger and larger, the silence carved out of the absence of feet pattering on the floorboards, of sardonic one-liners I overheard from my room while she flirted with this boy or that one, of quips to Sara or some other friend she'd never introduced me to, the elephant in the room began to swell, too, engulfing the house with all we couldn't speak of. It was then I thought maybe I needed to take more drastic measures. I only hoped it wasn't too late.

I wake up to pain.

It's not my swollen eyes that force me awake. My eyes have remained swollen since the first night she left, puffy as the flour-dusty balls of dough we snuck from Baba when he used to make our favorite, jiǎozi, from scratch at the breakfast table. It was the first night I'd slept without her since ... well, since ever. Before we were an inkling in our parents' minds.

This time it is my legs raging, the skin beating a new wound.

It's been years since I've torn up my legs with my fingernails while I sleep, jagged red lines working their way from calf to kneecap. I tried to stop it when it first happened—by wearing thick jeans I thought my hands couldn't conquer, swaddling my legs tightly in the folds of my comforter. I'll never forget when we had to dress in our hideous uniforms for P.E. in seventh grade after a particularly bad night. Kacey, the beautiful blonde popular girl, stood next to me to wait for teams: "What's wrong with your legs?" The class erupting in laughter, me cowering in shame. That feels so long ago now. I must have needed a release—from obsessing over the Lola what-ifs, Baba's threats, Mom's absence. Just, well, everything.

My skin pulsates. It's as broken as my heart is.

I look out the window behind my twin bed. The sun in the distance, another day I don't want to face. Another day without Lola. Another day wondering where she could be, whether she's okay, if she's safe.

Another day of wondering if she's just fucking with us. If this is all a big game. The possibilities are endless.

I stumble to the bathroom, my eyes barely open. I throw water on my face. The mirror is a reminder I want no part of. It's now or never.

I walk over to my bookshelf and crouch down. Tears fall on my hand that balances the rest of me on the floor. No object is safe from memory, or resemblance.

My bedroom wall is lined with a white wooden bookshelf Baba made for me in the backyard just after our tenth birthday. He built Lola one, too, identical to the one shoved against the bedroom wall that runs into the door. Cut from cheap plywood, the paint even but not as thick and creamy as we would have liked. The whiteness of the shelf stands out against the beige of the carpet, our walls. The shelves Baba made for his daughters are as identical as our rooms that bookend our side of the house on the second floor. Our rooms that bookend the house are as identical as we are.

As if identical wasn't bad enough. With mirror twins, the egg splits later than usual. If it had split any later, we could have ended up conjoined. Like Chang and Eng, forever attached. When the egg splits, it already has a left side and a right. Two embryos swim alongside their mirror image. I'm left handed, and Lola's right. We have the same little dot above our lip. Except mine's on the left, hers on the right. In some cases, mirror twins' hair might whorl in opposite directions or their first teeth might pop up on opposite sides of their mouths. Even their fingerprints could be mirror images of one another. In the scariest cases, one mirror twin is born with her organs where they're supposed to be, while her twin's organs grow on the opposite side of her body.

Although in the past we'd certainly been called every name in the twin book, especially by our older brother, Clark—Half Brain 1 & Half Brain 2, Tweedle Dee & Tweedle Dum, the Doublemint Gum twins, Add & Subtract, Plus & Minus, to name only a few—the distinction of our particular kind of twinning was a biological fact most missed. We weren't the same, although no one could tell us apart. We were opposites. And that meant that everyone saw us as the same person, two bodies with joined names, one personality with two faces, a coil of sameness. But how we saw ourselves was a whole different story. We saw ourselves as yin and yang, magnets with opposing poles that couldn't help but find their way to one another. At least, that is, until Peter and Paolo tore us apart.

We were born with some minor complications, but we'd soon discover it was the circumstances of our parents that placed us in the most danger. I was born at 5:30 on a Saturday morning in late January. Lola was born ten minutes later. I was born five pounds, fourteen ounces. Lola was born five pounds, ten ounces. The nature of our birth was yet another barb we traded back and forth, my tit for her tat. Someone, anyone, would ask: "How far apart were you born?" Lola would answer, "Ten minutes," her eye roll ready to launch, as I would retort, "More like ten years!"

Lola loved that she was the smaller one at birth. She would point at the baby pictures of us, standing in the bright summer grass, naked except for our matching puffy white diapers, insistent you could tell my bottom was bigger than hers, my belly rounder. We were like our own comedy act. I played the clown; she played it straight.

But something happened when the doctor pulled Lola out, which cast my story in turn. Lola's hip popped as she was being born. From that rift, our story spun. Her hip popped, which somehow came to mean that she was more vulnerable than I was, and that I must have kicked and kicked my way out. So that I could be first. So that I could get away from her and our tiny container of two. My four extra ounces at birth meant I was destined to be the thicker, curvier one. Lola's hip popping, which led to an X-ray to ensure the situation wasn't serious, spun her story, too. That she was broken, from birth.

If she was broken, I was whole. If she could break, then, by the very definition of mirror twinning, nothing could ever be wrong with me. Lola would become defined by the breaking of her body, a breaking that would result in feeling wanted, feeling seen. The fact that my bone did not sing of brokenness meant I would never want, or need, for anything. With that one little pop signaling her arrival in the world, the soundlessness of my own bones in that same room meant I would be marked as the invisible one.

I suppose we couldn't both have been the seen ones. We were twins. There always has to be an odd one out. The question of the safety of her body made her remarkable. For better or for worse.

When twins are born, each and every detail of our twinned bodies is held up to the light like a piece of someone else's mail you want to dissect secretly. Just the act of flashing a light through that envelope reframes its mysterious contents. The need to witness whatever is inside becomes an act of suspicion.

Twins are born, and without much question or choice, they become part of this thing much larger and snakier than themselves.

They become things.

But here's the thing. They don't even know it's happening.

But here's the thing. They don't know why it matters. And when they realize it does, it's often too late.

The bottom level of the bookshelf holds the pink Caboodle with the purple handle from middle school that Baba bought me at a yard sale (at first he wouldn't buy it for me since there was only one, which meant I would have something Lola didn't have, but it was an unusual scenario in which begging worked). It's next to my stuffed animals I'm too old to sleep with but not ready to permanently abandon (with my initials penned into their heels with red felt marker), and other odds and ends, like my favorite Monchhichi lunch box Baba got me from a trip back to Taiwan when we were little— things I want close to me but aren't useful enough to display more prominently.

Carefully stacked in the very left tucked at the back of the shelf is my prized stationery collection. I've taken it out when the occasion strikes—once in freshman year to write on pink floral to that Russian foreign exchange student Olga after she moved back to Kiev (I'd made friends with her mostly because no one else would), and a few times in tenth grade when Mr. Phillips (my eighth-grade physical science teacher) and I became pen pals for a while. I stopped writing after he started telling me how beautiful I was, how fetching he found my new glasses. Now a thin layer of dust clutching the edges of the plastic lids and the colored bottoms of the boxes reminds me how long it's been since I typed a letter.

But this isn't any letter. This one's for Lola. And the stationery on which I choose to write the story of our life, the secrets of our past, must be perfect. A letter typed on my laptop and printed on the family laserjet that rests on the small side table in the den isn't good enough. Not to mention too easily found by Baba's prying eyes. This letter requires being typewritten on my favorite stationery, which I keep at the very, very back of the shelf, so Lola won't take it from me. The few things that are solely mine become precious commodities.

But I'll give her a piece of myself if it means I can bring her back.

I gingerly pull out the box from beneath all the others. I smear its coat of dust into the air with the palm of one hand. I sneeze. Why has it been so long since I've written a letter, even if only for a reason to use my favorite stationery? The dust stings my eyes . I carefully wipe them with the fingers of my other hand.

I can see Lola now as if she stood behind me, scoffing at my stationery collection while secretly side-eyeing it in envy. Her usual. The paper is crisp, a sea of white framed by a black border (I'd bought it during my black-and-white phase). At the bottom of each sheet ballet-dancing men leap and twirl. The tininess of the dancers satisfies my love of miniatures, a predilection Lola and I don't share. I'm taken by the idea that dancers who can feel so grand, so beyond the world, can also feel so attainable in shrunken form on a single sheet of paper.

But that isn't the only reason it's my favorite in the collection. It's the row of dancing men.

In seventh grade, I took a dance P.E. class. It was the first time I'd ever seen Baryshnikov dance, in a film whose name I can't recall. There was something about the merging of the feminine art of the balletic form with the masculinity of his physique that turned my heart into a kaleidoscope of butterflies in flight. Ballet dancers weren't masculine the way men usually were, like football players or frat boys or courtroom lawyers. They were more malleable. Masculinity as expressed by a dancer is one of the few instances that doesn't terrify me. I've often tried to find that movie since. But I've never had any luck. A film that leaves that kind of impression on you never really stands up to its perfection in your memory. I remember Baryshnikov's double tour. It felt as if his body, upside down, twirling, twirling, was no longer within time and space, a spinning top with no gravity. His body in extended flight. His face perfectly still. He landed as seamlessly on the ground as he had been above it, noiseless and quiet, but a pretty quiet, like slumbering in a field of daisies in the midday sun. How fully I left that floor, spiraling with Baryshnikov in the blank spaces above my body. My first witnessing of fearlessness.

I tried taking ballet once. Even though I knew from the beginning it would be nothing compared to watching Barysh—I would be nothing. And I was young enough then, still small enough to fit the body type. I also knew because I was a girl, I'd never get to move the way men got to, take up so much space with leaps and powerhouse barrel turns. We started in the middle of a session, but Mom convinced Baba to split the cost for us to take dance lessons. Even Lola could tell how primal my need was to try it, so at first she went along. She knew Baba would never let me do it without her. Once a week we took ballet, tap, and jazz at the local dance studio. Our first recital, we danced jazz to "Walk Like an Egyptian," with red outfits complete with gold sequined headbands and anklets (Baba got angry when the teacher made us cut the feet of brand-new stockings we could barely afford to make them work with the anklets); tapped to "There's No Business Like Show Business" in matching barbershop-quartet hats with red satin bows tied to our shoes. Our dance teacher took advantage of our twinning by placing us front and center in that number. My favorite, though, was the

Swan Lake number. I was enthralled by the ethereal choreography, Tchaikovsky's transcendent score. I felt myself come alive as I fluttered my arms through the air as though they were wings. But, at the end of the season, the studio increased the tuition. Baba took one look at the sheet of updated fees, squirming his face into a question mark. "You girls really like dance class so much?"

Lola hated it. And her voice was the only one that mattered. So it was, and we no longer danced.

I remove a clean sheet of stationery from the box, place my thumb delicately on the little dancing men and trail it in a measured straight line across their gazelled bodies. I sigh in longing at their perfect, virile physiques. I can already imagine Lola's smirk from wherever she will open the envelope. Hopefully. I also try to imagine another scenario, a Lola who might want to hear from her twin, too. But. I can't think about all that now. I need to write from my own heart, my own truth. It's the only chance I have of winning her back.

I don't have mistakes to spare, so I address Lola in my mind first.

Dear Lo—, I write in the air before me.[1]

No. My stomach squeezes tight inside itself, a ripe lemon.

Dear Lolly, I try again. A million girls with lollipops, their cherry pouting lips. They invade my brain, burning. *No.*

I clear my throat. I bring each hand to my forehead, one meeting the other in an upside-down V, and rub my face downward. I run both hands through my dark cropped hair. The faded sides

1 "Lolita, light of my life, fire of my loins. My sin, my soul. Lo-lee-ta: the tip of the tongue taking a trip of three steps down the palate to tap, at three, on the teeth. Lo. Lee. Ta. She was Lo, plain Lo, in the morning, standing four feet ten in one sock. She was Lola in slacks. She was Dolly at school. She was Dolores on the dotted line. But in my arms she was always Lolita." (*Lolita*, Vladimir Nabokov)

glisten with sweat. I circle both arms back, open my chest, and let out a groan. A gust of air from the vent outside my room makes contact with my bedroom door, slightly ajar, slamming it shut. I jump. I tiptoe to the door, open it slightly, make sure it was just the AC. I return to my letter.

I roll a sheet very carefully into my vintage bubble-gum-pink Smith Corona, and deliberately hit each key, as though pressing each fingerprint in a block of ink.

June 28, 2019

Dear Twin,

Hi Lo. I don't really know where or how to begin or if there's even a chance this will reach you, that you will harbor enough hope in us to open these letters.

Love,
P

JANE
Avril

1

I lose myself in my thoughts for a while. I look down at the sheet of paper patiently waiting. This first letter is little more than a salutation. I need a change of scenery.

When I make my way downstairs, I hear Baba working in the garage. I find a stack of yellow Post-its in the drawer by the landline (who else besides Baba would actually still have a landline?), the same one he was glued to not so long ago trying to get a hold of Lola. I quickly jot a note and leave it for him on the breakfast table by the back door—*Hi Baba, Going to check out study guides at the library. Be back soon! Have phone if emergency. Love, P.* I slip out of the backyard on tiptoe, making sure to lift the latch of the fence gate with the smallest of movements so Baba won't hear and take his chance to interrogate me on where I'm going and what I'm doing.

I make it to the car. The air caught in my chest slowly fills the interior of my 2000 silver Corolla.

Free! For now.

I drive into town, which is Houston, a half-hour drive on 45 North. I'm going to Boomtown Café in Midtown to take my mind off things. As if it's possible. The barista at the register twists a mustache the color of the beaches of Galveston and looks at me with eyes that light up ever so slightly.

"Haven't seen you in more than a while," he drawls the way only Houstonians can, with a remote grin.

I recognize him, of course, because I come here regularly, and have for a couple years now, since Baba began to loosen the reins with us, if only somewhat. After he bought us each a cell phone so he could surveil us by constantly texting and ringing until we answered. Since Lola disappeared, he's been grilling me more than usual, but he hasn't said too much about my trips into town. I already agreed to defer college for a semester in the hopes that Lola might come back in the meantime. He knows he can't push me any further. "What if she doesn't come back?" is a question I always imagine I'll utter in response, but it's a cold marble trapped in my throat.

I smile and nod awkwardly while pretending to focus hard on the menu to avoid eye contact. It's anyone's guess whether it's me he hasn't seen in a while, or Lola. Before she'd gone missing she'd made it a point to hang out at all my favorite places. "You know you can't claim a coffee shop, right?" That's what Juniper asked the first time I tried to explain it to her. But it wasn't just my favorite coffee shops Lola was suddenly showing up at. For a while, it was almost weekly I'd hear from a friend in my Binders of Color group on Facebook that she was trying to reach out to meet up and talk writing. Sometimes she'd even show up to art openings and readings in town, hoping to use our face as currency, as a way in to the social circle I'd built over the past couple years.

At least, that's what she'd been doing before she left. She's gone radio silent on the other groups we share in common, but she could still be lurking around town, somewhere. I consider asking if he's seen her, but people get so weird when you bring up the twin thing. Anyway, maybe it's only me she's hiding from.

Just the other day, I read a line in a YA novel about twin college freshmen: "She couldn't single white female her own twin sister."[2] Until she could. Until she did.

I can't really pinpoint the exact moment it began, the paranoia that became a nightmare, the nightmare that became reality. I try to explain what Lola is like to people, but no one ever believes me. And it's not like they'll understand anyway. I try starting with the tiny details, but then I get the look—that I'm just giving them evidence that I'm delusional or worse, a hysterical, overly suspicious teenager. Those little changes in the atmosphere—that's where *Single White Female* starts after all. It's how the monster gets away with it.[3]

Besides, no one really wants to know what it's like to be twins. There's always that moment I meet a new person and they want so desperately to be told having a twin is like they always imagined: a best friend and a lover and someone "just like me." I can't be held responsible for the way their face falls when I tell them it's not all it's cracked up to be. And if they start by telling me "I always thought I was supposed to be a twin." Well. Then it's over before it's even begun.

When we were little, I wanted to be forever attached to Lola's side, mostly to Lola's dismay. I wanted to switch classes (and glasses) on April Fool's Day (Lola would never allow it). I never minded when we came out of our identical rooms dressed in the same outfit (Lola always forced me to change), and when we fight, I'm the one for whom the separation between us is a death, a lifeless limb, because the magical world of togetherness is gone, obliterated swiftly, pricking me like a dart. For Lola, I imagine, each fight that provoked our unbinding was a relief, a temporary escape from our bubble. In the worst fights that

2 *Fangirl*, Rainbow Rowell.

3 "You know, identical twins are never really identical. There's always one who's prettier. And the one who's not does all the work. She used me, then she left me—just like you." (*Single White Female*)

involved "fuckyou" and "Ihateyousomuch" and "bitch" and biting and clawing and pulling and clutching the other's body, we would run to our rooms, panting animals. I breathed heavily, my bursts of air sharp, quick. But then I became squishy again, painted with missing. I didn't know how to be without her. How could I when she had always been part of the air that surrounded me? I would sit on my twin bed imagining her sitting on the Lola version of that same mattress and tap my own foot impatiently on the beige carpet, waiting for time to run its course. I would always give in—it takes nothing for me to give in—and hop across the four feet of carpet to Lola's my-room, saying as nonchalantly as I could muster (my insides bouncing around like a toddler):

"Hey, what's shakin'?"

Lola's mouth a white line from the pressure her lips exerted to meet each other. "That's all you have to say? What the hell's wrong with you? You bit my boob, Poppy."

"I was hurt!" Water springing out of my eyes like oil spurting from the ground.

"You had no right to get mad at me."

"What does that even mean?! Emotions just happen, Lo!" Lola's white line a circle of dark for a moment to sigh, then back again. I, a sad cartoon dog, hang my head, retreat to my room, little sobs bazookas trapped in my chest.

Lola was born second. Lola's hip popped seconds after she was delivered, leading Mom to believe Lola might never get to bear children. ("They ran an X-ray over her girl parts!" Mom would exclaim as she told the story again and again. "With no protection from the radiation. Who knows what that did?") Lola can be a bully, which is why I (along with our brother Clark) love calling her Queen Lucy[4] to spite her. Lola blinks in all the family photos, rendering herself a blur in the frame. Lola is always without tears. (At least I've never seen them. Just before she left, Lola would tell me a story where she wept as though it was the dirtiest secret she could hold inside of her.)

But, this is the truth. We love each other. Our primary role in the family is to be those precious twins everyone coos and gasps at like babies, or old-time circus freaks . Besides, twins are always creepy, right? Didn't you see *The Shining*?[5] Baba dressed us alike so he could be a hit with his Asian immigrant friends and our white mother dressed us alike so she could attract more of her favorite foreign barflies and clubbers she loved to bring home, like turning her daughters into two gold fireflies held in a mason jar with a promise to release them into the starry night just as soon as she's caught the attention of her prince. But then she is so swept up with her prince she forgets the fireflies are still trapped in the mason jar on a coffee table in the other room gathering dust and the fireflies stay quiet hoping the longer they do the sooner the fireflies can become daughters again. And then the mother never really does remember the jar, the fireflies, the starry black night that is their home or even her daughters, so in the jar they remain until the prince breaks their mother's heart and leaves her, which he always does, and she needs them again.

But, while they are waiting to become human, to distract themselves from their mother's occasional and recurring disappearance,[6] or their father's unthinking rage, the twin girls

4 Van Pelt, *Peanuts*.

5 "Hello, Danny. Come and play with us. Come and play with us, Danny. Forever [shot of bloody Grady corpses] and ever [shot of bloody Grady corpses] ... and ever." (The Grady Twins, and did you know there's actually a film production company called Grady Twins Productions?)

6 I was a woman that needed to be wanted by adults. (One of the apologies our mother sent, during one of the times she left.)

giggle underneath their thrift-store quilt on their double mattress in their mother's small apartment as they perform twin impressions of their father's Mandarin[7] for fun[8] or at least try to, incomprehensible as their father's language is to both of them. They record themselves on their mother's old boombox singing and acting out *The Little Mermaid*, their favorite, and then play back the recording while pointing at each other and giggling, their two faces turning as red as the pair of suckers their mother brings home from the bank. They hold each other in the bed they share while they wait for their mother to come home from the club, desperately hoping that their mother will come upon them, soft and sentimental in her tipsy haze, and clutch her hand to her heart at the sight of her twin girls and their doubled love.

"Hey Pops! Over here!" Kai waves me down, breaks me out of my reverie from where he sits at the bar. I welcome the chance to avoid any further engagement with the barista.

"Hi hon! Whatcha up to? Oh my god, let me see this outfit! I call first dibs on those shoes if you ever grow out of them."

Kai's in his usual fabulousness of gender fuckery, a bright pink hat, a mustard silk tunic over blue cargo pants, and bright green oxfords. Half of Kai's family is from Thailand, the other half from Mississippi. He is my love's best friend .

"Aw, boo. You're the sweetest. Let me check out all these pins! Girl, GIVE ME that Lena pin! And Baldwin! And Ali Wong! I'll take all those for my hat, please and thank you."

We queer-coo at each other back and forth for a few minutes, and it's just the break I need. The bartender working today's shift, Violet, is our favorite, white, but super genderqueer and chill. It

7 You'll notice, perhaps, that our surname, Uzumaki, is of Japanese origin yet Baba speaks Mandarin. That's because Baba's half-Chinese, half-Japanese, and his parents met after Ojiichan moved to Taiwan when Baba was a baby.

8 Cryptophasia refers to a language developed by twins that only the two children can understand (*crypto* meaning secret, *phasia* meaning speech).

snaps me out of my Lola stupor, even if only for a moment.

"Hey Poppy, what's it gonna be? The uje?" They wink at me as they twist the little hairs of their undercut with the fingers of one hand.

"Actually, it's so fucking hot out today. Make it half-iced, half-cream. And can you grab me the avo-benny?"

"Mmmm, now you're making me hungry. Bring it right up!"

While the bartender leaves to put my order in, Kai leans over and affectionately scratches the shoulder of my denim jacket.

"Pops, tell me what's what. June told me about Lola. That sounds in-tense. How you holding up?"

I take a breath.

I grab Kai's hand. It feels so comforting knowing I can do that with someone who will never take it the wrong way. Like the way I always imagined families to be.

"You're so sweet to ask! I don't even know how to talk about it anymore—"

"Oh, honey. You absolutely don't have to if you don't want to. But just know I'm here for you. And you know Juniper is. Whatever you need. We can sit here and talk about bullshit, or we can sit here and not talk. Whatevs."

Kai draws me into a hug, and I can't tell if I'm crying because of what's happening with Lola or because of Kai's words. It's probably both.

We break apart and I wipe my face with my napkin.

"Thanks, Kai. That means a lot. I just feel like I need to do something more dramatic, you know? Because, like, she's still not fucking home and Baba's not doing enough. At least, not enough for me."

"Yeah, I totally get that. So what does that mean? Do you have any ideas?"

I feel a little guilty to tell Kai before I've had the chance to tell

Juniper about it. But I think she'd understand that I need people to talk to.

"Actually, I do. I'd love to hear your thoughts actually. I'm thinking about writing Lola a series of letters and mailing them to that P.O. box she kept after ... well, you know. I bet she still has it. But to lay out for her my side of the story, how I saw that whole mess with Peter and Paolo, and just all the family shit. And you know, hyper–Virgo moon, so I'm thinking I'll write eighteen letters, one for every year of our life. Just put it all out there and see if it'll break through to her somehow. What d'ya think?"

Kai takes a beat, runs a hand through his short black hair. I can tell he is thinking through it all, careful to respond. Classic Gemini, measuring out all the sides.

"Wow. That's a lot. But I love it. It feels right to me. I think, if anything, you'll know you did something, you know? And that's gonna do a lot for you, to work out all the shit you can't with your parents. 'Cause, boo, no offense, but you didn't exactly win the parent lottery."

We both giggle. Our laughter cuts through the air with a light touch, like spooning that layer of skin that settles on cooling soup.

"So, I'd love to hang out with you, but I kinda think I need to give you space to work this out? But check in later if you wanna go thrift-store hunting or hop down to the roller rink. You know I'm always down for either, just text me!" Kai gives me a kiss and flits out of the café, leaving me alone with my thoughts and the letters I haven't yet written.

About an hour later, I look up from the book I'm reading.[9] A busboy has already cleared everything but my watered-down iced

9 *The Perks of Being a Wallflower*, Steven Chbosky.

coffee the color of caramels. I wheel my stool towards the front of the café and gaze out the window overlooking the patio. My eyes barely focus on a commercial playing on the television just in front of the glass. I try to redirect my attention but my eye catches it. Two young women: identical faces, identical straight blonde hair, identical argyle sweaters, identical grins. I rub my clenching jaw as I try to stop the reflex action it has taken too many times.

I sheepishly pull out my large yellow Moleskine, well aware it's the sort of notebook that automatically aligns me with those #amwriting types I try to dissociate from. At least I have an excuse. My left-handedness makes it impossible to use spirals unless I want to mark my wrist with little red indentations. Of course Lola got to be the right-handed one. Just another perk of being a mirror twin. Lola uses Moleskines, too. Of course she does. Because I do. As far as I know, Lola still uses the reporter style that opens vertically so anyone seeing her use it in public would think, *Oh, you know Lola? She's a Writer.* Who could blame her? That's the most Lola can hope for. Since everyone else knows the truth. That I'm the twin who writes. Always have been. At least, I hope they still remember .

Who am I kidding? I know how this started. *This* being Lola. *This* being Lola mirroring me (in ways beyond our faces and bodies and designated outfits). *This* being Lola acting out. *This* being broken Lola trying to break me, too.

It started with Peter. Paolo came second.

I stop myself. I need to start the next letter before my mind travels to the darkest caverns of our story.

I open my notebook to draft while I'm away from my typewriter. So that I don't waste even an ounce of ink.

June 28, 2019

Dear Twin,

I know this is the worst cliché ever, but what's happened to you also happened to us. Your story is part mine.

I hope, maybe, if I tell you my side of the story, maybe you'll come back and then everything and everyone else who tried to fuck with us and wedge their way between us won't matter anymore.

Here's the truth. I miss the version of me only you know. I miss the Poppy that has a Lola she calls home. And I miss you. It doesn't feel the same since you left.

I know so much has happened. But, with these letters, I hope I can help remake what's been broken. I want you back.

I know you think I hurt and betrayed you - as you've put it, "more than any other person in your life." I hope one day you'll see how I've been the only person in the world who ever tried to protect you.

Okay. Enough with disclaimers. Here's my side. I hope one day to hear yours.

Love,
p

2

I put my pen down, take a beat. My phone dings in three ascending notes. My blood itches beneath the skin. I'm afraid it's Baba, texting to ask where I am, or demanding I come home, threats he doesn't form but that hover in the air between the words, like a wasp waiting to feast. But my phone delivers me a different message—it's Words with Friends: *Juniper Kim sent you a message!* My skin now jumps for the most opposite reason.

I hurry to slide the screen over with my fingertip and enter the lock code. Suddenly aware of the other faux writers staring at me, most likely provoked by the intrusion of my phone's audible ding on their writerly work, I set the phone on vibrate. The stares return to their rightful positions on all the various-sized screens of their matching laptops. I pull my index finger down to refresh the game, waiting for Juniper's move to announce itself, her message to arrive. Yet another new word Juniper has suddenly discovered wins her 118 points. I groan aloud. Instead of entering in my next game move, I click on the message:

> Koala! How's your last chance to win over the heart of your evil twin going? Any new strategies? If anyone can melt the ice cold heart of Dr. Evil, it's the cutest little Popcorn in Movietown, USA!

My mouth is an orange slice of joy.

I look back at the words scrawled to Lola in my notebook, but now I'm also occupied with thoughts of Baba, my chagrin at having to report everything back to him in immigrant speak, removing all the juice and glitter of the English language in every sentence I speak to him. He's been in the States for twenty years, ever since his mother had—as he puts it—"ship me on plane to Kentucky"—or, in other words, sent him to America from Taipei to pursue a training program in carpentry, but he understands his children easier if they speak in the fragmented English that mirrors his own. I get it, but it remains a burning wish that he would have spoken to us in the sounds of his home. It would be so much easier, on all of us. The separation our languages cuts between us is an ocean of unfamiliarity that feels impossible to cross. How can I ever fully know him when our minds and hearts don't speak the same? It's even more painful when I watch him chitchat with my stepmother in Mandarin. There's an ease and a sweetness it brings out of him that I'll never know. As I message back Juniper in our own abbreviated tongue, it isn't lost on me how I adore our back-and-forth silly banter that often fragments in the same way Baba needs to understand us. I live for the intimacy she and I build through our own speech, a kind of twin language that isn't marred by all the shit that surrounds Lola and me.

Things aren't easy for Juniper, either. She's a visibly queer Korean butch in Clear Lake, the tiny suburb south of Houston where we both live. Would we ever get to live out our own rom-com, floating on our own pink cotton-candy cloud away from the world? Lola's enough for Baba to handle without me adding to his stress by coming out. It's hard to imagine what he'd do if he found out my "study trips" were just veiled secret rendezvous with a girl. Not just any girl. A Korean girl. Whenever we get tofu soup in Chinatown, Baba takes no time at all to lecture us at length about how "the Koreans so violent!" I've always found it rude and ungrateful, TBH. Projection much?

Once I started seeing Juniper, though, it grew even harder to hear. It didn't help I knew Juniper's mother used to beat her. When Juniper didn't ace her calculus test. Or took too long in the bathroom. Or refused to wear a dress to church. When I express my frustration at Baba's generalizations, Juniper always says: "I mean, can you blame them? Korea's always been at war."

But that's how we found each other. Because we see something of ourselves in each other. What it means to have no choice but to hold your parents' demons. But, when it comes to Lola, well. That's a different story. Juniper's an only child so it was hard to explain what it means to be a twin. I've never said this to Juniper, but sometimes she acts jealous of the space in my life Lola occupies. As though Lola takes away the mirror between our own queer pairing. I never bring it up, though. It's impossible, for both of us. Even if I brought it up, what could either of us say to make it less true?

I finish typing in my message, press SEND.

> Hey little panda, UGH. She probably doesn't deserve this much attention. But, I gotta try, right? I'm kinda out of my mind with worry. Miss you, boo! Wanna go to Hermann Park and blow bubbles at the koi in an hour before I turn into a pumpkin? Do have new strategies! Wanna tell you all about it! ❤

I consider adding a snark about her ridiculous word but decide against it. After spending a minute or two gazing at the photo of us on my home screen, I look back down at the letter. It's not Lola's fault she doesn't have a Juniper. I think at least a dozen times a day how Juniper brings a previously unknown happiness to my life, a feeling I'd always associated with the rich (and white) (and straight) people on TV. I'd long made peace with the fact that the life I watched on television just wasn't in the stars for me.

And then I met her. Juniper Hae-Won Kim.

I'd seen her around school before. She was hard to miss. A Korean soft butch with hair so black it shone blue, cut short like a boy and slicked back like a boss. Every day she wore a short-sleeved black button-down to school, loose-fitting jeans, shiny patent-leather chucks. Whenever I passed her in the hallway, she made all the little hairs on my arms stand straight up.

I wanted so badly to approach her, find out everything I could about her. But she felt so legit gay, maybe even lesbian, and what was I? I'd never kissed a girl before, although I used to read Harlequin romance novels in my closet long after Lola and Baba and Clark had gone to bed, imagining myself in the role of the big-chested man, and that it was me passionately pressing my chest against the heroine, stroking her face with one hand while I kissed her. Until I saw Juniper, I always imagined that my fantasies would stay a dirty little secret. I never thought they'd ever become real life. Until there she was in front of me, and all my thoughts turned to her.

One day, just after the final bell rang, I saw her slip through the wide halls in between the masses of chattering white cheerleaders and football players and mean girls. Without thinking, I awkwardly ran after her in a slow jog, quiet and just far enough back that she wouldn't be able to hear me tail her out of the building, but still keeping her within my sights. If she turned me down, or fled from me in disgust, I didn't know how I'd get home. I'd already missed the bus. But I couldn't spend one more day not knowing who this mystery girl was.

I struck up a conversation with her in the breezeway outside the front entrance. I can't even remember what it was I started with, but I know I bumbled and rushed, my breath spilling out in between each word, my heart racing faster than my speech could catch up with. I think she knew. Why wouldn't she? I had no game. Her lip curled in a tiny smile, and I hoped it meant what I wanted it to mean. This was the first time I'd ever talked to a girl wanting more, and I had no idea what I was doing.

Before I knew it, there we were, leaning against the trunk of her car in the school parking lot, Juniper's hands shoved into her back pockets, mine clasped together behind my head, the heat beating on our dark hair and the asphalt underneath our feet, geeking out over all the things I'd never been able to share with anyone before. Like Malinda Lo and Alice Hom and Sandra Oh and Hayley Kiyoko and that boy in BTS with hot pink hair and how hot Juniper would look suited up like Gosling and how stunning (she said it, not me) I'd be in Fenty and Janelle Monáe and Tessa Thompson and Karen O and Mitski and how her biceps slash lez hairstyle reminded me of Justin Bieber, but in a good way. And then we had a petty sesh about how straight white girls are the WORST, especially the ones who think they're so woke. And then she poked my hand with the softest touch, like a dragonfly, and asked if she could give me a ride home. That's when I knew.

In any other universe we would have been inseparable after that day. But in a small suburb where queer teens don't exist except in the closet and with two queer Asian girls who have helicopter parents with a fierce hand, it took time. It also took time to reassure Juniper I wasn't just another straight girl using her to fulfill my gay fetish, make out with her once in her bedroom while her parents were at work, and then bully her at school the next day so that no one would find out about it. Juniper's the butch, the exposure, the one who can't hide. All I know is that when I lie in bed at night and think about Juniper's fade coming to a half-circle at the nape of her neck, her arm grazing mine in the seat next to me watching *Moonlight* on our first date, my body is ablaze.

Being with Juniper is so different than being with boys. They turn me on, too, sometimes, but the switch Juniper flashes on in me twinkles like a sprinkler in the hot Texan summer. She isn't like anyone I've ever known, not like Lola or any boy. With Juniper, I'm wanted. Safe. Seen. I knew the only way to get to Juniper's heart, once we met, once I knew I was head over heels, would be if I did it. I had to. A week after our conversation in the parking lot, I snuck a note through the slats in Juniper's locker, using, of course, my favorite stationery. (This is, TBH, the real reason I don't tell Juniper I'm using the same stationery for Lola's letters. Juniper will only be hurt by it, and what for?) The note asked Juniper to meet me at a park bench across from the Menil, our favorite museum, to attend a teen book club on *Giovanni's Room*. When Juniper arrived, she held a curled fist in her back pocket, the other nervously smoothing down her hair, a black leather satchel draped loosely across one shoulder. I wore a nude shade of lipstick, a floral hairpin and paisley bow tie, and my most flattering A-line dress. Before Juniper could utter a word, I placed my hand delicately on her cheek. From that moment junior year, we just fell into each other. Like magic.

Juniper teaches me all the pop culture I've missed out on during the years of Peter and Paolo, the years of trying to save Lola, the years Baba kept us on such a tight leash. I show Juniper how real girls love. She teaches me all the queer pop-culture secrets—the queens and the butches, the trans men and femmes and enbys and genderqueers. I don't always get all of the queer-coded references Juniper lines her text affections with every day but I love trying to figure them out. Sometimes I try to play it cool, but Juniper always knows. And she loves it almost twice as much when I don't get the reference, when I just "Mmhmm, totally!" along hoping Juniper won't notice. News alert: Juniper always notices. She tousles my hair and giggles at me as if I'm some adorable fuzzy creature from outer space that landed on her doorstep and thinks her doorknob is a pillow.

I'm anxious. I click the screen on my phone to see the time. 12:30. Only half an hour before Juniper picks me up, and she's always early. So Asian. Actually, it's one of the things I love most about her. Baba's always on time, but Mom, during her good spells, was always inconsistent—sometimes on time, sometimes twenty minutes late, sometimes hours late, and sometimes hours late and then a phone call saying she wasn't coming. At least, that's what it was like before Lola disappeared and Mom moved to Arizona. But with Juniper, it's different. If she's ever late, it means something far worse than lateness has happened.

I rub my eyes. I roll my shoulders back. I take a breath.

June 28, 2019

Dear Twin,

I passed by the Sunbeam factory on Washington today. It was always your favorite. I thought about what you used to do when we'd pass it, how dramatic you'd get when you'd take a big whiff of those bready yeasty fumes, and how we'd laugh. We'd giggle for so long we couldn't tell which laugh was yours and which was mine. Our laughing as big as the factory itself. It made me cry. I hope wherever you are, you're laughing that big-hearted laugh. Big enough for two.

Yours,
Poppy

3

As I finish the third letter in my notebook, my lap begins to vibrate, startling me. I look down at my phone. A text from Juniper: Come hereeeeee pleeeeaassseeee! It makes me giggle. I clumsily close my notebook and grab my pen. On my way out of the café, I drop the pen several times. First, it knocks against the ruffles of my skirt and then in the space between my neon-pink oxford and my baby-blue men's argyle socks until it ultimately lands on the floor. I try to pick it up, but the pen pops out of my hand and onto the very thick greasy folds of hair of one patron who is very seriously posting a comment on someone's Facebook feed about how annoying Lena Dunham is. I roll my eyes and smirk to myself as I delicately try to extract my pen from the woman's thick bouffant hardened with product. It's not until the woman clears her throat that I realize I'd stopped, mid-extraction, to read over her shoulder. Her eyebrows scold me.

"Oh, sorry, I..." I begin, but then my phone buzzes again with an exasperated text from Juniper: Hurry it alreads! I leave the woman's glare where it is and scurry out the front door without finishing my apology.

Juniper sits in her 2005 Accord, nestled precisely against the tree-lined curb. Her father got it for her on sale at CarMax. We'd had enough debates about whose mode of transportation beat whose: her Accord versus my trusty Corolla. Running out of breath and googling reviews on our phones, the argument always ended at a standstill. We felt a certain comfort at the Asianness of it all—our matching hanging air fresheners from the same ten-pack (for one dollar) we bought together in Chinatown, our mismatched dents we inherited with our pre-owned cars, hers on the front right, mine on the back bumper. I hop in the passenger seat.

Juniper grins her classic tiny grin as I hoist her bulky bag into the back seat. I straighten my skirt beneath me, fold the ruffles in my lap so they don't get caught in the door as I shut it behind me. I clumsily struggle out of my teal bolero, chucking it in the back seat. Finally settled, I notice Juniper's amused side-eye in my periphery.

"Uh, yeah, bro?"

Juniper smiles wider, her teeth showing. "What what, little koko?"

"Just what's so funny, anyway?" I furrow my brow, readying myself to be on the defensive.

"Nothing! Sheesh! Just think you're cute, that's all."

Juniper kisses me quickly on the mouth, pulls at my earlobe. I sigh. The kiss resets me, reminds me there's a life outside of home. Or that there's finally a home outside of my life.

I decide to wait until we get to the park to tell her about the letters, once we're lounging in the grass, cradled by the park train with the squeals of small children passing by, the koi ker-plunking back and forth next to us. I'll wait until we're eating cheese and crackers on my favorite *Spirited Away* blanket we keep in Juniper's trunk for any time we can escape to meet for a quick picnic in the park or a nap in the sun on the Menil lawn. Juniper gets a lot of pride out of being the masc of our pair, which means she always drives. I don't mind. It makes me feel cared for—and she knows how anxious Houston traffic makes me and my terrible sense of direction. I show my gratitude with the little things—unlocking her door from the inside after she lets me in but before she makes it around to the driver's side. I saw it in a movie once—that that's how you know if the person you take on a first date likes you.

I always spread the cheese on the crackers for her, too. I learned to offer food watching Baba do it for us at home or out in Chinatown, even when there was a lazy Susan so we could reach the food ourselves. The work of preparing food and offering it to another person was always the way Baba showed us love, and it gives me great pleasure to offer it to Juniper in kind. Juniper always teases me that she can feed herself—"I'm a grown-ass woman, you know"—but I know she secretly loves it, especially here, when we are twenty-five miles away from home, from the prying eyes of the kids at school or our parents. Our own little island. Today Juniper brought added gifts: kimchi in a tupperware, bāozi in a paper carton.

"Bāozi! Panda, where'd you get these?" I'm too excited to wait for her answer. I grab the puffy bun, still warm, and tear the paper off the bottom and bite into it. The pork inside is juicy and familiar, and without Baba's hovering presence, it tastes like home. I exhale the steam out of my mouth and grab a pair of disposable chopsticks Juniper empties on the blanket, pick a tangy bite of kimchi to balance the pork. Heaven.

"I grabbed them at the bakery on Bellaire on my way over, for the little koala! I thought you could use some food therapy," she says, winking while she lovingly watches me stuff my face. "So, tell me this new idea of yours. What you cooking up this time?" Juniper hooks one thumb into the pocket of her blue jeans while swinging her carabiner around her other thumb. I pinch out another helping of kimchi, offer it to Juniper while I swallow. She leans towards me, grabs it with just her mouth and grins as she crunches on the pickled cabbage.

"Yeah. So, I had an idea I wanted to tell you about. I ran into Kai at Boomtown, and told him about it. So please don't get mad when he talks to you about it! But it was really great. He really gets it. Anyway, I want to write her to give her my side of what happened where she'll hopefully be in a space to listen—about our childhood, about Peter and Paolo. And of course, 'cause I want to make sure she's okay. I'm so worried, to be honest, especially after she didn't respond to Baba or any of my texts. But I've been thinking maybe I'll cut myself off at eighteen letters—you know, one for every year we've been alive together. And if she doesn't respond after that, there's not too much else I can do. But at least I know I'll have done something. No matter what happens." My eyes smart, so I shove another bāozi in my mouth. I don't want the only time I get with Juniper to be me crying. Which has been a lot lately.

"Oh, bear. I'm just so sorry this is happening. I really wish you could just live your life, instead of it always being about her. But I get it. This shit is super tricky. Even though you have such a complicated relationship, I know how much you care about her. I do worry about the toll all this shit takes on you, Pops. It's been so hard on you already. It's not like she's been the kindest to you to begin with."

"Yeah. It's just hard. It's so fucking complicated. But she's still Lola. She's still my twin. It's not her fault this happened to her. Which is sort of the reason she's like this to begin with. Sigh."

A moment of tension hangs in the air between us, an opaque cobweb. Before Lola left, she'd often been a sore subject for us. Juniper knows how insecure I was at first about Juniper choosing me instead of Lola. The fact that Lola's straight, or that they've never even met, didn't matter. What mattered is I wanted Juniper to want me even if Lola pursued her. Because when you share the same face with someone you can never feel safe.

Just before Lola left, it had gotten to a point where I brought it up so often Juniper would tense up if I even tried to ask for reassurance about it. She'd get frustrated by my lingering doubts, or when she could sense I was trying to keep her from ever crossing Lola's path, accusing me of not trusting her. I tried to explain. It wasn't about trust. It was about twins. It was about the fact Lola was always the one that was picked. Why would this time be any different?

"I know. I mean, I can't imagine what it's like for you. But I think it's a smart idea. It seems like there's a lot you need to say to her, that's never been said, that might be holding her back from coming home. Who knows? You need an end to this mess, once and for all. For your sake as much as hers. So do we. God, we've got to get out of here, and if this is a way for it to happen where you can still feel good about it, I'm all for it. Also. I think having a cut-off number will help you know when to stop. For. The. Love. Of. God."

I giggle at her emphasis in spite of myself, which only makes me giggle harder and faster and higher pitched until my eyes begin to water and I fall backwards, the top of my head grazing the grass where it lands just beyond the blanket's reach, Chihiro's unblinking eyes staring into the nape of my neck. As the giggles subside, I listen to the birds quarrel and the koi splash. Juniper scooches next to me on the blanket, cooing at me and cradling my head like a football.

When I get home, Baba's nowhere to be found. The note's still on the breakfast table, so I crumple it up and shove it into the pocket of my skirt. I tear out of my oxfords without untying them, popping the heels off with the opposing foot (like I learned from watching Baba), and kicking them into the shoe closet. As I take the stairs two at a time, exhausted but also anxious to type up the letters, I consider going back downstairs and arranging my shoes in the closet as he would like. I leave them as they are.

I glance at the black alarm clock on my dresser, its red numbers blinking the time at me like a countdown: 4:00. Baba doesn't usually start making dinner until a quarter after five. That leaves just a little over an hour to myself. Baba's a carpenter. He makes Asian-inspired wooden furniture he sells independently—bamboo benches, platform beds, shelves, folding screens, etc., that he learned from Ojiichan when he was younger. He spends the rest of the time on Uzumaki Productions, a paper theater company he codirects with his friend Ming. The productions, which focus on Chinese adaptations of Western classics, are constructed entirely out of paper silhouettes projected onstage using light and animation. Since Lola left, Baba's been much more obsessed with his current work in progress. Based on the furtive glances he shoots me every time I peep into the garage to check up on him or grab a soda (Baba stocks the fridge with only caffeine-free versions), I'm guessing his next show might be an original that has something to do with Lola. I wonder if he's told the other company members what he's working on yet, or if he plans to throw it on them at the last minute. It's hard to imagine how they'll go for it given that Peter, who used to be part of the company, is one of the reasons she's gone—and the other members, mostly Taiwanese, just want to save face, sweep what Peter did to Lola under the rug. Even Peter's own wife acts this way.

Even when dinner doesn't come with its usual lecture, I always lose the feeling of safety and freedom once 5:15 rolls around. I have to be ready for anything. A snack missing from the pantry, the remote for the television downstairs misplaced under some couch cushions, a bad mood that prompts him to search for problems in me to act it out on. One moment I'm lounging in my room, finally starting to relax, and then, the next thing I know, Baba's shriek shoots up the stairs, white and hot and shattering. A tornado. I never know if it's going to come with his hand striking my skin. Sometimes the threat is just as terrifying. Thinking about it turns me white hot with rage, too. At Lola, for leaving me alone with him. She knows what he's like.

I turn on the old TV in my room. I'm always amazed it still works—Baba's had it since when he went to college.

I press PLAY on the DVR of *Mr. Holland's Opus* that I recorded off cable, fast-forward until I find my favorite part, the part that always makes me cry. The sweet-faced girl with a bright orange ponytail holds her saxophone as it glints in the daylight that streams into the band room from the skylight. She wants to quit band. Mr. Holland asks her what she likes best about herself when she looks in the mirror. The girl with the orange ponytail says she loves her hair because her father says it reminds him of the sunset. Mr. Holland tells her to play the sunset, and then, of course, she plays the piece all the way through, without a single mistake.

And just like that, I'm lost in longing, lost in hopeless wishes I could have a teacher like that (who didn't also turn out to be a creep), lost in wishes for a father who would say something that beautiful to me and it could be true, but also lost in wishes Baba could tell me anything about myself and that it would be true only of me, not of us. Even this fantasy can't be shocked out of my daydreaming, reminding me once again that when one is born a twin, one is refused the one word any baby desires over all others. I feel so childish thinking of it now, even in the recesses of my mind, even in the most private of places. But I can't help it. I whisper it to myself, and as I do, the word croaks from the tears trapped in my throat.

Special.
I keep going, breaking through my own dream.
You are never special. Not even your first breath was your own.
I weep until I exhaust myself, accidentally falling asleep.

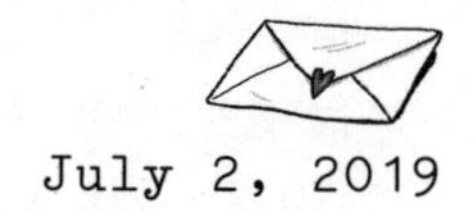

July 2, 2019

Dear Twin,

The other day while Baba was at a meeting, I let curiosity get the best of me and looked in some of the old photo albums. The photos are still there, but where Peter's head used to be there's just a big empty hole cut out. I just thought you would like to know. At least that's something, right?

Love,
P

4

It's been a week since I typed the first three letters on fresh sheets of stationery and sent them to Lola.

Every day I check the mail while Baba works in the garage, claiming I want to make things easier on him during this difficult time, but it's really so I can intercept her reply, just in case it comes.

It hasn't come.

Every bill or piece of junk mail I hold in my hands as I walk the block and a half back to the house from our mailbox is a reminder of the emptiness I feel without her here, no board to sound off on, the only way I've understood myself.

July 8, 2019

Dear Twin,

The other day I was reading that book about the high school boy who writes letters to a friend he doesn't name. It's about him coming to terms with being a freshman, but it's also about him coming to terms with his aunt's abuse - I feel so anxious reading it, how he speaks around what happened with his aunt as we get closer and closer to it by the end. He never really does come right out and say it, though. And then when he finally talks about it, there's so much terror about what she did to him, how it broke him in the process. No matter how many times I read it, it always makes me cry.

Anyway, there's this part in it where Patrick, this gay senior he becomes friends with, finds out the boy has a crush on Patrick's stepsister, and explains girls to him. He says to the boy, "Girls like guys to be a challenge. It gives them some mold to fit in how they act. Like a mom. What would a mom do if she couldn't fuss over you and make you clean your room?

And what would you do without her fussing and making you do it? Everyone needs a mom. And a mom knows this. And it gives her a sense of purpose. You get it?"[10]

And I got so sad reading that part, because it reminded me of Mom, or you know, how we always wanted Mom to be. But she just couldn't. It just wasn't the way she was built. Like what Baba said. "Most mothers bond with kid. Your mother never could." I thought about the photos of her with Clark when he was first born. Little baby Clark swaddled in a yellow baby blanket. Mom's face the color of mother's milk. And then I thought about the stories Mom used to tell about her brothers in Kentucky, how they used to bully her. I thought about how Mom always called Grandma bonkers and mean as a drunk and how she used to say "I bet she caught the diseases of half the nutjobs in that mental hospital where she used to work as a nurse." Ugh.

I mean, what's a mom who doesn't fuss over you and make you clean your room? What mold did Mom fit herself into? Or maybe she'd done the opposite, spent her whole life trying to claim any mold

10 *The Perks of Being a Wallflower*, Steven Chbosky.

but the mom one.

Or maybe it was having daughters that did it. Not just any daughters. Us. Twins. I always wonder if she subconsciously named us after two different versions of herself - Poppy because she always imagined herself a red flower among the green grass, Lola because Lolita was the first novel she read entirely in Russian (at least, that's her story, even though we know she dropped out of college after freshman year when she and Baba met). Half flower/half nymphet.[11] With a flick of her wrist, she cast both her twin girls as things. And that was only the beginning.

Maybe we'll never know the truth behind our names. Was it because she wanted to live a short explosion of a life, blood red in intensity and like fireworks, beautiful and red hot and going, going, poof, gone, before anyone had the chance to see her decline, start to wilt? Maybe that's why she idolized Marilyn like she did. Remember when the walls of that one apartment she had were draped in photos of her dressed

11 "We are not sex fiends! We do not rape as good soldiers do. We are unhappy, mild, dog-eyed gentlemen, sufficiently well integrated to control our urge in the presence of adults, but ready to give years and years of life for one chance to touch a nymphet." (*Lolita*, Vladimir Nabokov)

in black negligees and red lipstick in famous Marilyn poses? Or when she would record birthday messages for us on her own voicemail in a perfect "Happy Birthday, Mr. President" impersonation? God, that was so embarrassing. Or that phase where she dyed her own dark hair blonde with peroxide, shedding the discarded bottles all over the house as though she wanted everyone to know she used the same chemicals as the blonde bombshell who died so young, so tragic, so beautiful. Like a bad Lana del Rey song.

I always wonder what she was thinking when she named you after Lolita. What mother would name her daughter after the most famous girl-child in all of literature, after a young girl molested by her stepfather? It's hard not to think about now, after what happened with Peter and Paolo. I mean, I guess we can't blame her. How could she give her daughters a life she could never allow herself to have, since she never confronted her own scars? She had two little girl bodies she was responsible for shaping, all while still trying her damnedest to run from the shadowy form of her own saddened girlhood haunting her. When she looked at her reflection, did her beauty serve only to mock her?

Did she imagine instead what everyone would really see if they knew the truth? Is that why she always ran?

I don't know - sometimes I feel sorry for her. She was a victim, too - I can't imagine what it's like to find out your stepfather molested you and gave you tranquilizers to prevent you from remembering it. To tell your mother, and have her refuse to believe you. But I don't know, knowing she'd been through it, it just pisses me off even more that she'd subject us, you, to Paolo and all those other men. Why wouldn't that make her want to protect us even more?

Oh. Maybe you don't know this yet. Mom took off the minute we discovered you left.

At least she said goodbye this time. She came to the back door, told me she had to go see about a job in Arizona. That she couldn't wait any longer for you to stop playing with people's emotions. I tried to tell her. That she needed to care about what happened to you. That I needed her help finding you. But she just did her usual, interrupted me halfway through and said she couldn't deal with this. "I'm gonna have a mental breakdown if we keep talking about this shit," she muttered to herself as she backed away from me and got into her car, slowly driving out of my sight.

I guess now we know where you got it from. But, she's the mom. Isn't it her job to stay? Why aren't we enough to keep her?

5

Lola pumps her legs back and forth on the swing set, coughs loud enough for the teachers to hear. Lola's sick, so she gets to see Mom on an unplanned visit, since Mom can always figure out a way to get the afternoon off. When she answers the phone, anyway.

Lola pulling my best friends aside, exposing my most unflattering moments, causing all of my friends to pull away from me. Lola intercepting notes I was on my way to put in a friend's locker, finding out my boy (thank god) crushes, threatening to reveal them to the entire school. Lola flirting with them in the hallways until they fall for her, then rejecting them—"I'm just not that into you"—chuckling with a friend as she takes off running, mocking their wide-eyed devastation.

I make it to the cafeteria at lunch hour only to find Lola's replaced me at my own table with my own friends who avoid my eye contact. I try to find out what happened. When they see me, they run the other way.

Lola mocking my laugh—"Why do you laugh like that? You always scrunch up your face. It makes you look weird. Don't you want boys to think you're pretty?"

Lola shaming my weight—"You know the other night I had a dream you were pregnant and you didn't look that different."

Me running home to tell Lola about a ten-minute run-in conversation I have with my favorite poet at a café downtown, the poet who wrote a book about being queer (she doesn't know this about me yet) and having fucked-up parents too, which made me feel less alone. The poet who I tell about being a twin and about Baba surrounding us with all of his friends from Uzumaki Productions who only speak English when they have to but he never taught us Mandarin and so we just stare and stare at them in our language darkness. When I tell the poet all these things he says, "Could you dream up a better life to give someone who would end up a writer?" He signs my book, which I always have on me, *I can't wait to read your book some day. xo.* After I finish my story, Lola laughs and laughs and laughs: "Is there a point to this?"

I grow smaller and silent, the room (and Lola) swelling bigger and bigger until it (and she) snuffs me out.

But. But.

Lola's voice as she impersonates Ursula in our recordings on Lola's phone. Lola as she hides under the blankets with me while we make nonsense sounds in Baba's voice pretending to speak Mandarin. Lola performing the best Clark impression. Lola sneaking out of the house with our Hello Kitty bank money, booking it to the supermarket, and returning with a long sweaty squishy package of chocolate-chip cookie dough, two plastic spoons, two glass bottles of Coke, two bendy straws (blue for me and pink for Lola). I suppress a giggle while eavesdropping on Lola lying smooth as silk to Baba in the living room, imagining the cookie dough moist from condensation weighing down her pink satchel causing it to dangle lower than her hips, the bottles clanking against each other quietly as Lola holds the bag carefully against her body so as not to arouse suspicion. Lola heel-toe-heel-toes up the steps (the quicker the feet, the greater Baba's suspicion we have something to hide) until she finally makes it to my room where we spoon out the dough quick and itchy, washing it down with soda through our straws until we see ourselves in each other, our faces and hands and mouths ravenous for sugar and delight, and barely put down our guilty pleasures on my desk before we collapse backwards on the carpet, giggling and licking our sticky mouths and undoing the top buttons of our jeans while we rub our swollen bellies overwhelmed by such a rare and glorious feast.

July 13, 2019

Dear Twin,

The reason I'm writing these letters is because I want you back. But I'm also writing you because I want you to know what it means to be your witness. What it means to watch men break your twin while your parents do nothing to stop it. What it means to watch your parents choose themselves and their own images over protecting their daughter. They chose guilting their other daughter, me, into being the watchful eye, over doing it themselves. I'll never get that.

But since you've been gone, I've been thinking so hard about what it is I got out of being the witness, or the savior. I just didn't realize it at the time. How, as long as you were the problem, the broken one, then I got to be the good one, the one who could fly right. Maybe you thought you won when Peter and Paolo picked you. I can see how powerful that can be. But I know I got to have a different life because it wasn't me they wanted. I wasn't chosen as their prey. I never became soiled through conquest. Talk about survivor's guilt. I know we don't exist on an even playing field. That even with the same body, the same face, the same childhood, because of them, we'll never be equal.

Damn. What a rip-off twinning turned out to be.

Love,
P.

6

Sometimes the world's just too much.

By the time I wake up, Baba's already texted me that he'll be at an all-day meeting with a big furniture client. I take advantage of his absence by leaving another note on the breakfast table that says I'll be studying all day at the library downtown. I send a quick text to Juniper before I jump in the shower .

> Could you Venmo me twenty bucks so I can grab a coff and croissantwich, pretty please, Pandabear? I don't want Baba to give me grief about how much mons I'm spending!

I check my phone while I finish getting ready—Juniper's added forty dollars to my account (with coffee cup, croissant, rainbow, and double heart emojis in the memo). Because it's through her church, Juniper's parents let her tutor the young kids after school and even let her keep the money in her own account. Baba's given me an ATM card attached to an account he puts my "allowance" in, but it's only for emergencies and I always have to ask him for approval. I send her a gushy text composed of only emojis, hop in the car, and head to Epicure.

Of all the little cafés in town, Epicure's my favorite. Close enough to the gayborhood, but one of those places that brings no specific customer, a place Lola wouldn't feel was hip enough to add to her list of places at which to set up camp all day and pretend to be a writer. It still feels all mine. At least for now.

I love the dainty silver pots of French-press coffee the server brings to your table, the too-sweet homemade berry lemonade made during the unbearable Houston summers, the long and bountiful display of French pastries—everything from strawberry napoleons dusted in powdered sugar topped with strawberry slices to éclairs (which I never order because they remind me of every ballerina-turned-bulimic Lifetime made-for-TV movie I've seen—it's always the éclair glittering on a Manhattan street corner that initially does the girl in), macarons made in every color of the rainbow to fluffy pistachio cake. I love the croissant sandwich I always order, the sunlight that pours through the windowed wall I always sit next to. In Epicure, I imagine I'm in a different world. A world that, apart from what I have with Juniper and Kai, doesn't have to feel so heavy and sad and always, always, always hard. Hard with a neon capital H. My little French café makes me feel warm and light. Like I'm anywhere but here.

On my drive over, two pigeons, entangled, tango ahead of my windshield. They unnerve me. I jump in my seat, worry they'll smash against my car and die right in front of me. I wonder if this is what happens to teenagers who've been terrorized by their parents too long. The world seen in horror slow-mo, composed only of potential catastrophes. Luckily, the birds claw their way back into the air and fly away.

I try to shake it off, focus on making my exit off 45. I'm about to take Allen Parkway, my favorite road in Houston. If you hit it at the perfect time, it can be breezy and uncongested, especially at 10 a.m. on a weekday, where it doesn't trigger my claustrophobia.

Except today. My exit's blocked. I have no idea what to do.

It always frustrates me when I can't adapt to things, remain chill at the sight of trouble. I know any other well-adjusted eighteen-year-old with normal parents could easily find their way out of this situation without thinking twice about it. It reminds me of that time in seventh grade when I had to get a ride home from a teacher I was helping with an after-school program and I couldn't figure out my way back to Mom's house. We weren't like other kids. We didn't get to ride bikes or even walk down the street. The teacher didn't get why on earth I couldn't find my way home. We eventually had to look it up on her phone. She told my mom when we got there, since it took so long to finally make it back. After we said goodbye, Mom went off on me, telling me how pathetic I was, how fucked up we all were because Baba never let us go anywhere. I cried myself to sleep that night. She came into my room and held me, trying to apologize after she'd calmed down from her own embarrassment and saw what her words did to me. I craved her affection too much to reject it, even if she was the one who'd caused it. By then the shame had already set in to my veins and nothing she could do could take it away.

After I take the next open exit and pull over to the curb, flashing my hazards, I resist the impulse to emergency text Juniper. I don't want to be that kind of girlfriend. I don't want her to feel she has to be everything my parents aren't. Anyway, it doesn't seem fair to ask for something I know I can't return. But, luckily, Juniper's not the only person I can call to bring me down from a meltdown.

I call Cendrillon, my chosen fam, my friend anchor, my surrogate mama.

Cendrillon answers on the second ring.

"Hi Cend," I'm barely able to say into the phone before my throat turns to liquid from crying.

"Poppy? You okay? What's going on?" Cendrillon says in her

calm, steady voice, one I'm grateful to rely on when nothing else around me feels stable. Just hearing her on the other end of the phone immediately slows down my pulse, bringing me back to a sense of myself that felt so far away just moments ago. I empty out to her as she patiently listens on the other end. It's only when I've finished, when she's said the simplest but most sincere things—"Oh, Poppy, that sounds so difficult and overwhelming. I'm really sorry that happened."—that I realize it's all I actually needed.

Cendrillon is this incredibly beautiful, very wise woman. Her name means "of the ashes." It means "one who has a deep inner desire for love and companionship, and wants to work with others to achieve peace and harmony." It fits her perfectly. After all, she's helping me rise from the ashes of the wreckage of my own burning house. Slowly, she's teaching me how to find peace within myself, to help create it for those around me. Cendrillon's a French woman in her early forties with dark hair and glittering emerald eyes.

We first met at a ballet performance downtown. This was in sophomore year, in between Peter and Paolo, at a time Baba and Mom were trying to give Lola more attention in hopes they could distract her (even though it was never Lola who was the problem in the first place). It kept the heat off me for a while, long enough that I was able to go into the city unsupervised to see performances like this one, leaving early enough so I could score a student rush ticket.

It was my dream to collaborate with this particular company on a production of my own design, *Frankenstein* recast as a twin narrative. I'd been rereading Shelley's masterpiece ever since AP English class that year. When I first read *Frankenstein*, it felt like Shelley had taken my world and just collaged all the pieces together. It had the narcissistic father (although I always liked to think of Frankenstein as the mother) who abandons his child because of how his child's image mirrors his fears of his own monstrousness. It had the theme of contending with one's inner monster. It had the twinning between Frankenstein and the creature. It had the self-educated outcast, once eager to discover the world, made monster by the very people he'd tried to nurture and love. What if there could be a *Frankenstein* ballet that dealt not only with narcissism and the monster and abandonment, but also with society's fear and preoccupation with twins? Could I pitch this idea to this company, and possibly collaborate on the production, too?

I didn't want to blow my one chance to make a good first impression. To prepare, I'd read everything I could get my hands on that dealt with *Frankenstein* at the library: the feminist work of Mary's mother, the backstory that inspired her to write it, the work of her husband, the poet Percy Shelley, the psychological underpinnings you could attach to the story, and basically every single connection to *Frankenstein* I could find. I also researched any kind of literary or artistic portrayal of twinning I could find online. I even had a shelf in my room dedicated to this project. Only when I felt I had done enough research (Juniper would probably have to be the one to determine that this was "ENOUGH, set it up, bro!"), and only then, would I craft out a storyboard (hopefully with Clark's help), and bring it to the director. That is, if I could manage to get five minutes in front of his face. Who knew what would happen from there. But it was a dream, one I wanted more than I wanted almost anything.

After our first meeting, I'd come to learn that Cendrillon worked as a counselor for the French-speaking students at Awty International School. At night, she was active in the arts community. After the performance that night, I was milling about in the lobby, not quite sure how to schmooze with the high-art rich white people oohing and aahing about the show, name-dropping a dancer here and there. It was obvious I was not one of them. But I wanted desperately to become one of them, no matter how I looked to them in my pink oxfords and orange-and-blue pinstriped suit layered with a ruffled baby-blue shirt and a striped bow tie, or how invisible I tried to make myself so I could more easily eavesdrop on the conversations I wanted so desperately to be part of.

Cendrillon was the type of person who could feel the energies of those around her as though she were a psychic (like a real one). On the night we met, Cendrillon very elegantly, very nimbly (her legs long and thin like a gazelle's) lessened the space between us. Cendrillon was soft in her gait, but swift.

"What did you think of the performance, dear?" Cendrillon inquired, direct and nurturing.

"Oh, it was just exquisite! Didn't you just adore it?"

I tried to sound as I imagined this mysterious and marvelously adorned creature would want me to sound. If I could become the thing this person wanted me to be, which to me meant to frame myself in the words and body language of the person in front of me, then I might have a better chance of the person sticking around.

"Listen. You don't need to worry yourself putting on airs with me. I've seen you here before, and I know you want a place here. Can we meet for tea and chat? It's too crowded here. I can't concentrate with the moths swirling, can you?" She placed her hand on my shoulder, and gave me the tiniest smile.

I sighed with relief. This woman hadn't just wanted to be adored by this young little wallflower. Cendrillon had gotten me instantly. And intimated, just a bit, that it was okay for me to be myself. It was far less taxing not to work so hard to emulate another to be accepted.

Cendrillon placed a business card with her cell number written on the back of it into my trembling palm, leaving behind a small coral lip print on my cheek and the scent of tulip-tinged perfume, and strode away as quickly as she had arrived.

From that point on, Cendrillon became a kind of mentor, a guide for how to wade through my emotional abyss. She didn't seem to mind we never really talked about what was going on in her life, even though I would try to inquire from time to time. We spoke about the latest art-house films and sometimes we would go to other dance and theater performances together. When we ran into each other, we smiled at each other from across the room, the exchange like holding the same little flower bud in each of our pockets. Cendrillon was wonderful to rant to about the latest findings for the *Frankenstein* project, what little connection I'd found the company might be drawn to, what backstory the director would find less interesting. And Cendrillon was an older, wiser woman to cry with, to empty my hardships onto. Cendrillon had never had the chance to have children since the only man she'd ever loved had died of cancer early in their marriage. She never really did recover from the loss. So, perhaps there was something in our connection for Cendrillon, too.

When I first told Juniper about her, Juniper was wary and protective. She worried Cendrillon had ulterior motives or maybe had a young-woman fetish. But once Juniper met her, she got it. "She's like your art mother," Juniper declared. "I think she's just what you need." And she was.

I take my phone out of my backpack and click on Waze, placing my foot lightly on the break. I wait impatiently for the app to load, the muscles in my body flexed, and I don't feel my foot slide off the break until my car beeps repeatedly as my tire runs into the curb, setting off the antilock brakes. I jerk the steering wheel and park the car next to the curb, forcing myself to breathe, pushing the little ball of my belly down as I exhale.

I imagine sitting at my little spot in the café next to the big window, opening *The Astonishing Color of After* to where Juniper and I had left off at the park last week. I picture the boutiques in the shopping center across the street I'd browse after my breakfast to find the perfect outfit for our last night together before Juniper's trip to Northampton planned around her campus visit to Smith, the send-off gift I'd make sure Juniper left with so she'd have a reminder of something from home.

As the tears streak down each cheek, I try to stop the shame spiral from descending, try not to blame myself for how sensitive I am, for being unable to change my route, for being so inconsolable at why something so trivial is so hard for a girl like me. I think about how hard it was for Lola and me to love each other in all the mess of what Baba and Mom gave us. I wonder if Lola and I will ever overcome the curse of our family, if we'll ever be okay. Maybe Lola had it right—maybe the only way to survive it is to leave it behind.

After I cry it out, I pour some water into my hands from a leftover Ozarka in the cup holder and flatten the cowlick at the back of my head. I roll my shoulders back. I scroll through my fifty favorite photos of Juniper in my phone and finally get the new directions to Epicure. I put the car back in drive and continue to the destination.

July 17, 2019

Dear Twin,

D'you remember when Mom had us all summer? And worked all those weird jobs to pay rent - retail at Stride Rite, assistant manager at The Body Shop until they found out she'd fibbed on her resume and fired her, receptionist at Twilight's salon for, like, a week, waitress at Giovanni's? Or how she'd give us the penny jar every time we were dying of boredom so we could walk to Wendy's and get Frosties? God that was the worst. Having everyone watch the cashier count 107 pennies each out of that jar! Ughs. Or when she was too high to go out, and she'd throw some food stamps at us so we could walk to Kroger and get milk and eggs for the morning? That summer was such a mess, but it's one of my favorites we ever had together.

Oh, and then remember she was cleaning houses some weekends that summer, too? You never wanted to go, but I always felt bad for her, so I went a couple of times. You know how I hated saying no to her. Sigh. I tried to draw the swirls from the fancy marble linoleum in my sketch pad, and had the most amazing bubble bath. I felt like Julia Roberts in Pretty Woman. I really had no idea fancy people lived like that. Wow. My skin soft as a newborn. Creamy soft.

This one time Mom fed us lunch from a can of caviar - there were, like, a hundred perfectly stacked cans in the cabinets, and she insisted they'd never miss just one - and a box of crackers that tasted super expensive. They didn't even leave crumbs when you bit into them. That's how you know.

That house had a pool, too, and a burgundy suede sofa that felt like silk. It was heaven. I was always a little sad you didn't come to that one. You would have loved it!

That was the summer Paolo started sending you letters. When we came home that day, he was sitting on the couch in the living room, and you were hanging on his every word, swinging round and round the banister from the kitchen while you bantered back and forth.

Love,
P

7

I log on to Instagram. My username's golightlyintothatgood-night (half Holly Golightly / half Dylan Thomas). There's no identifiable information on my profile—I never know if Lola's stalking my comings and goings. I want her in my life, but I've learned my lesson about sharing anything public Lola could integrate into her life as though it's hers for the taking. People always think they know you if they know what you look like, so looking exactly like someone else makes them doubt you. And once that doubt's there, it's hard to go back.

Besides, I only use my Insta for Juniper. We share little image love notes that hold symbolic significance only for us. We both keep our accounts private—there's no telling who else would find out about us and out us. We know how tiny the world can be. It's just not worth the risk. It makes being stuck home (except for our little secret trysts here and there) not feel so isolating and lonely, and it's fun trying to come up with new ways to Insta Juniper with little inside jokes and symbols of affection.

The evening before Juniper's flight out started with an early afternoon text.

> Wanna tell the Grudgesters you're spending the night at the cabin to study? I'll tell DMZ I'm having a sleepover at Kai's.

The Grudge and DMZ are our nicknames for the most violent of each of our parents, giving a special nod to their countries of origin. Juniper came up with what to call Baba after we watched the Japanese horror film of the same name when we first got together. I'd just finished telling Juniper Baba's story, the one that revolves around his dominant Taiwanese mother and passive Japanese father: When he's young, Baba's father works at a bank and Baba goes to private school. One day, his father, who Baba always says was too impressionable, goes to the casino to play poker with some colleagues. He loses and has to pay them back. He embezzles the money from the bank, an amount so small it would have normally gone unnoticed. But the banks happen to run some standard checks on the system the following morning. He's arrested for bank fraud. Baba can't attend private school without his father's income. As Baba told us once, his face contorted into discomfort and pain, the family "loses face, we never recover." Baba never got over it. He still carries rage at Ojiichan for subjecting the family to such disgrace. And Nǎinai, forced to support the family on just a schoolteacher's salary, became hardened and cruel. As Mom used to tell us all the time, Baba married her just to spite Nǎinai. Baba had written her saying he'd met a white girl, Nǎinai had written back saying that Americans have fifty percent divorce rate. They married a week later. Wasn't it Anne Carson that said you can't have rage without sorrow?[12] And so, the nickname stuck.

The DMZ is shorthand for Juniper's sharp-tongued mother with a fierce hand, who used to beat Juniper if she refused to wear a dress to church, or when she cut her hair without telling her first. She's why Juniper wants to fly halfway across the country to attend college so she can finally be her fullest, most

12 "Why does tragedy exist? Because you are full of rage. Why are you full of rage? Because you are full of grief." (Preface to *Tragedy: A Curious Art Form*)

sincere self. Juniper's father is around, but he lets her mom run everything. DMZ is the border between happiness and entrapment, harmony and panic.

Kai wants to leave, too. Once he's freed from the clutches of his sweet but clueless parents, the first thing he plans to do is find a way to get cheap T and save up for top surgery. Until then, Kai makes do with a buzz cut and a binder. Even though they don't get it, Kai's parents leave him alone for the most part. Because Juniper met Kai at church, Juniper's mom never protests when Juniper and Kai have sleepovers. Thank god. It's the perfect alibi for us to get away from our parents.

Baba's never thrilled when I claim I'm spending the night out, but if I get him on a good day, when he's distracted enough by work, he'll usually says yes. I'm ecstatic when Juniper texts me, my pulse tripling in speed. I'm nervous—a sleepover is the rarest of occasions (obvs), and even though we've already slept together, just a couple of times, we're still figuring out the ins and outs of queer sex with each other. Juniper's a stone butch, but as she says, she's trying to be "more relaxed about it all." She doesn't want me to feel I always have to be the bottom, the receiver, the one open to the acceptance of another body. And Juniper knows I've already had some difficult sexual experiences with boys that left me feeling violated, like I was just a vessel for whatever they wanted. Juniper had one girlfriend before me—she was white and femme. It didn't last long. I've never been with girls before her, so I often feel shy and insecure to initiate anything.

The last time, in a hotel room just outside Austin (when we both claimed we were on a school trip and had fake permission slips to prove it), Juniper asked me if I'd be willing to try more than just fingers. I blushed, turned my face away and covered it with both hands. She took me into her arms. That's when she whispered in my ear, so sexy, that she had a strap on she'd never used before. She hadn't felt safe enough with her ex to use it with her. "So," she said, curling a tendril of my dark hair around her finger, "this could be a thing we'd learn together."

Would this night be the night we'd take the plunge? I'm excited about the prospect of another way to be intimate with Juniper, but more than that, I'd love to give Juniper a new experience for once. Shrouded in the safety I feel with her, I wonder if it will feel like the best of both worlds, the sensation I've had before, but with Juniper's tenderness and sensitivity? My heart is a chorus of tiny tapping feet.

If it's with Juniper, then nothing is everything and everything could be nothing and still everything. But I'm a planner (super Capricorn), so I better be ready for the occasion. Just in case.

It's 3:00. The plan is to meet at Kai's at 4:30, before his parents get home. We always try to follow the alibi all the way through, even if there's no parent to witness it. It also gives us time to hang with Kai and have some pie and ca phe sua da at the house—Juniper didn't want him to feel like we're using him. This means I better get ready for an hour of teasing and elbow nudging between Kai and Juniper about our hot date before we head out.

I know it's a lot for Juniper to take this time out of prepping for her campus visit and impeccably organizing her suitcase. She makes me feel important with the smallest thing, without even a reminder.

July 25, 2019

Dear Twin,

I'm not the girl that gets picked. Not for softball in P.E. in eighth grade, not for high school dances with boys, and not for Most Outstanding Student or Most Charming and not to sit next to in the cafeteria and not for, well, anything. Ever.

If anyone gets picked for things, it's you. Even Peter and Paolo - although what they have to offer I wouldn't ever, ever want, but still, when it came down to it, they still picked you. After it all happened, you told me you asked (of course you asked) why you. Why not me? That's the twin question, I guess. TBH, I would have been too scared of the answer.

"Poppy's too goofy," you told me they both said.

If it were me, I'd be too scared there was no answer, that we were interchangeable, and you just happened to take to it first.

But, there is someone in my life. Someone who proves, after years of searching for the right way to live, some way to make something whole out of all the rubble of our tragedies, I've finally gotten it right. I finally got picked. Someone stayed. I just wish I didn't have to also lose you in the process.

Love,
P.

8

Juniper drives us an hour out of town to get to the small cabin Baba bought years ago, when property was still cheap, but has been vacant since Lola. I practically bounce in my seat as we flee Clear Lake and the gap between home and our destination lengthens like a string. Juniper's left hand holds the wheel, the other rests on my thigh, exposed by the shorts I wear.

"Hey honeybunch," Juniper starts, her gaze now unflinching at the road ahead of her, "you wanna stop at triple eight?"[13]

I glare at Juniper. "HA HA HA. NO WAY am I going to risk running into Baba and his colleagues—they meet there regularly!"

Juniper giggles, tousling my hair, then brings her attention back to the freeway.

Farther along the route, we stop at a little diner across the street from the beach for a quick bite of salmon burgers and fries. They taste like ocean air, salty, windswept, sun-kissed. After dinner, Juniper parks the car along the sea wall. While I roller skate[14] on the boardwalk, taking photos of the world as it whizzes past me or a blurry self-portrait with my Pentax, Juniper strolls closer to the water's edge, gathering seashells and

13 888 is the only Szechuan restaurant in Clear Lake. They serve eggplant in garlic sauce, and a fried salty fish dish Baba always orders off the menu, and my favorite, gān biān sì jì dòu, dry-fried green beans. I slightly resent I don't feel safe enough to stop there.

14 Although I only roller skate for fun, I have to have the best pair. I save up the allowance Baba gives me for a year to buy a pair of aqua Moxis. They match the ocean.

taking digital shots with her Nikon of the shore or the beach-goers lounging in the sun. I hope there's a way we can collaborate one day, if we end up at Smith together. I wonder if Baba will ever let me go.

I love how we can be together together, but also alone together.[15] It's not easy for me to rewire my brain to think outside the codependent bubble of twinning. How do you when that was how you were brought into the world? But I do need a space of my own, a place where I can define my own ways of being, and healing.

I give Juniper her care package as soon as we settle in. Comfy in my Princess Mononoke pj's, Juniper in her loose-fitting boxers and black tee, we sit cross-legged facing one another as Juniper opens her gifts. I can tell Juniper's nervous as she fumbles with the wrapping paper. It's hard to be an Asian girl accepting gifts. We never know how much gratitude to express to the gift giver because too much would only fill the giver with discomfort. But, nevertheless, it's my goal to get her a gift that's good enough to make her blush.

She opens a box of strawberry Pocky (her favorite), a pink T-shirt I bought online from the Brooklyn Museum that reads *gender is a drag* in lowercase (just the kind of thing a Smithy would wear), and the latest Sarah Waters novel.[16] I also give

15 *Singles.*

16 One of our favorite novels we read together, along with watching the BBC adaptation on one of our first dates, was *Tipping the Velvet.* We had a giggle fest with Waters's euphemism "spendings," like the line, "When I reached my crisis I felt a gush, and found that I had wet her arm, with my spendings, from tip to elbow—and that she had come, out of a kind of sympathy, and lay weak and heavy against me, with her own skirts damp." Since then, we always refer to any potential sexual encounter as "Hey, can we have spendings soon?"

Juniper an old iPod Touch loaded with our favorite love songs.[17] Juniper turns her face away after scrolling through a few, her eyes sparkling like Sailor Moon. The more they sparkle, the shier but happier I become, shuffling my feet and casting my eyes downward like a wallflower in a *Peanuts* cartoon.

"Oh, little koala! I adore them. Thank you," she whispers, her eyes darting away from mine.

Juniper pokes me in the ribs, declaring, "Okay, my darling little popchip. Now your turn!"

I let out a confused gasp as Juniper hands me a gift bag wrapped in rainbow ribbons. "Junebug! But why? I'm not the one going on a fancy college trip!"

Juniper smiles quietly. "Oh, don't think I'm letting you get away empty-handed! Also, just a little something to cheer you up while you do all the Lola ughs," she winks as I look down at the bag on my lap.

I put an incredible amount of thought and attention into my gifts for Juniper—it gives me much pride to do so—but I never know quite how to receive them from her. Gifts as a child were always fraught with performance anxiety and twinhood. Either Lola and I received a single gift as though we were conjoined or we received the same outfit in different colors. This always caused us to fight, as we always ended up wanting the same color. To keep us from fighting, Baba started to hold each gift behind his back and then he'd make us each choose an arm and then, when the gifts were revealed, scream "That's it! No fighting!" before there was a chance to thank him.

It's hard to know how much to exclaim my excitement, or the

17 Janelle Monáe's "Make Me Feel," the song Juniper first did a little dance to for me in her bedroom when her parents were out of town, Indigo Girls' "Power of Two," and Skim's "She Said," a Korean queer hip hop artist who we saw perform at Avant Garden on one of our first dates. For starters.

inverse, how ungrateful I'd appear if I said nothing upon receipt of whatever it was I was given. Mom was the opposite, having come from the culture of loudmouthed white Kentuckians, and so she, in not so many words, demanded a kind of performance that couldn't help but feel insincere in comparison. Mom couldn't afford much so luckily I didn't have to display how appreciative I was too often. But, as a result, it means I'm pretty nervous receiving gifts, because of how overwhelmed and undeserving I feel. It's also hard to imagine I could be known by another so well that I'm often moved to the point of expressionlessness. Everything inside of me could be fireworks, but on the surface I'd look as still as a frozen river.

My hands shiver as I tear apart the wrapping. Juniper asks me to open the first two together. One is a small bag of gummy candy with EVIL TWINS in big yellow-and-red lettering on the front, illustrated with a boy in red wearing glasses and a bow tie bound to a devilish boy in yellow with spiky hair and gritted teeth. The cartoon bubble next to the boy in the bow tie says "I'm sweet!" and the one next to the boy with the spiky hair says "I'm sour!" The back of the bag lists the twinned flavor combinations: Angelic Orange & Mischievous Lime, Sweet Strawberry & Rowdy Blue Raspberry, and Charming Cherry & Wicked Lemon. Next to the gummies is a Blu-ray of the movie *The Bad Seed*.

"See Iconapopgoddess! Evil twins! Hopefully this'll help you get to know more about the villain you are trying to crush and also convince to come home!" Juniper giggles.

I try to stop the tears but they never listen. As I grab Juniper and cover her with tiny little wet kisses all over her neck, I feel them dampen her T-shirt.

"Aw, little Pops," Juniper pulls me away from her to peer into my face.

"Oh, it's wonderful. I just. I'm just ... so touched I just don't know what to do. No one's ever loved me and known me like you do. No one's ever given me things that were about me and not about them. I just ... sometimes don't know how to be with it, that's all."

I shift around so my head rests on Juniper's chest, and as Juniper strokes my hair, we both gradually doze off.

We wake up a couple of hours later. Outside is hidden in darkness. We begin to kiss, short and rough kisses at first that grow longer. Our lips still joined, Juniper slowly stands up, gingerly taking my hand and leading me to the bedroom. I'm often struck by how holding Juniper's hand feels like holding my own. It's soft and slopes in the same places. The twinning of queer bonds is never lost on me, but in this case, it gives me comfort instead of grief.

Unclothed and in bed, we fall on and against each other, our dark beige bodies certainly in the same family but not identical. My Mannerist torso, her boxy waist. The same long Asian nipples but Juniper's broad and flatter chest against my slightly fuller one. Lying on my back, I relinquish all control as I try to relax myself open, Juniper easing her hand in slow movements until it entirely finds its way inside. We gasp, but for different reasons. After I climax, Juniper whispers, "Do you want to try it now?" I'm nervous but more at ease. I smile and nod without speaking. Juniper scurries off to the bathroom.

I can hear lots of squeaking sounds of rubber and silicone from the bathroom, where the door is slightly ajar, including grunts of exertion. I giggle.

"You okay in there?" I inquire, trying to suppress my laughter.

"It's NOT funny!" Juniper huffs back. "You wanna try?" she

adds defensively.

"Panda! Come here! I help!" I offer as a loud snap of material slapping skin erupts from the bathroom.

"There!" Juniper declares triumphantly. "No, that's okay, hon. Got it! Here we go!"

Trying to explain what it's like, or how it's different from penetration sex with a boy's body, feels impossible, like trying to translate an expression from one language to another. Regardless, it's like getting everything that turns me on all at the same time, but limitless. I feel closer to Juniper as though we're both in it together, rather than being so strictly relegated to giver and receiver, top and bottom, Juniper as much in it as I am. And it can go on for as long as we want it to .

I'm a little put off at first by the purple of the strap on until Juniper reminds me how weird it would be if it were flesh colored. It gets to be its own thing, separate from men. After we finish, the strap on abandoned on the floor and Juniper fast asleep, I'm so content. It's the perfect intimate moment for us to share before Juniper leaves, something I already know I'll play in my head again and again to cope with missing Juniper while she's gone.

July 25, 2019

Dear Twin,

I don't even know how to begin retelling this story, THE story, the two strands of a single body interwoven like DNA to inform who we are, how we move through the world, and how who we are is made up of the you and me we leave behind. But, I know I have to write this story down for us, my version, and how I experienced what happened, for us to have any hope at being an us again.

But. I'll be honest. I've been dreading it. I've been distracting myself with other things - anything so I don't have to go back down that road. The first time was bad enough. And it didn't even happen to me. I can't possibly imagine how it feels for you. But, here's the thing. You got out. I'm still here, stuck with the aftermath, staring into the emptiness of Baba's eyes that this tragedy left in its wake. As always, here I am, the placeholder for your mess. And, as usual, you're nowhere to be found. At least before, you always popped up, even in the places I never wanted you. Now all I want to know is where you are, if you're okay, what you're doing, what you're thinking.

This is the moment. These two stories. These two halves of one narrative. They changed the course of our story. Every single thing that comes after this is because of this moment. I hope it will help. To see what I saw.

As you read this next letter, try to remember this is just my account of how these men entered our lives, my interpretation of the consequences of their destruction. Not yours. I can never know the world as you know it. And I promise I'll never assume that. I just ask you do the same.

I have to go. Baba's calling. I can't believe you've been gone two months already.

Love,
P

9

Questions I wish I could ask Baba:

Why didn't we call the police when I told you about Peter? Why haven't we filed a missing persons report? What did you do to Clark to make him never to want to come home? Why do you hit people when you don't get your way? If you hit us when we do things you don't like, why didn't you hit Peter? Lola's been gone two months. Why do you act like it doesn't matter?

July 25, 2019

Dear Twin,

Peter was first. In the beginning, he loved us as if we were two halves of one whole, two sides of one coin. We were used to that. But we adored him anyway. He was like that shūshu that always teases you to show you affection, or the Baba we never had. I mean, Baba was his scariest back then. I have the diary entries to prove it, how afraid I was that one day he'd land me or you or Clark in the ER from one of his rage spirals. It seemed like every day he was going off the rails, calling us "you fucking assholes" or threatening us with "Man, sometimes I just love knock the shit out of you," his voice somehow more threatening than the hand he raised above our head when he said it.

Peter was such a relief from that. When Baba made us come to Ming's house with all the others whose language we couldn't speak, dressed in our matching purple velvet frocks and Mary Janes, Peter was the only one who knew English well enough to want to talk to us. At least, that's what I thought in the beginning. That he was humoring us, these poor twin girls with no one to talk to for hours while Baba swam in a sea of language he never taught us.

I mean. He taught us pinyin so we could write down the English equivalents to the sounds of the lyrics for contemporary Chinese karaoke songs in our song binder. He coached us on how to sing them, so we'd be ready when it was karaoke time at Ming's house each Saturday night. Peter was the dj. We hovered around him like bees to nectar. We didn't know to question the things he said, like "Man, if I your age, I would knock down the door to be with you girls." I didn't notice you get closer and closer to him until later, didn't pay attention to how your stockinged thigh rubbed against his free hand that wasn't working the karaoke machine.

Baba loved the attention we got from Peter, and from the others. How many men fawned over our twinned beauty. He loved taking the credit. And we thought it was a good thing - maybe it would make him happier, maybe we could keep the beatings at bay if we worked our charm. Because Clark was a boy, he didn't have to come to the parties at Ming's house, didn't have to learn how to sing karaoke for Baba's friends. Funny, isn't it, how it's always the girls that end up being endangered, even though they need the most protection?

Each Saturday, Baba hung the dresses on our doorknobs an hour before it was time to leave. His wife usually met us there later on, after she spent time with her own children. After we changed, Baba would rifle through his wife's jewelry, grab two identical strings of pearls and fasten them around our throats. He'd place the pairs of black Mary Janes side by side downstairs by the back door. This was how he groomed us for the grooming Peter would ultimately extend.

Peter's flattery was the links of chain enclosing us. At some point, I grew uncomfortable with my infatuation with a man I saw as an uncle. I even wrote about it in my diary, and reframed how I saw him through my confused, adolescent eyes.

And then one day, he called you on the landline while Baba was at work. You didn't know I was on the other phone. He said: "I had a dream about you last night. That we had ourselves a little slumber party. Are you up for it?"

That's when everything changed.

p

10

Juniper's only been gone a few hours to Northampton, but I already feel as though the ground is less firm beneath my feet, as though each moment that passes is another one that slips through my fingers like smoke. It doesn't help that Smith's known for being a lesbian mecca, doesn't help that that's the reason Juniper wanted to enroll there in the first place—free from the cishet world we've lived in so long.[18] What if she meets someone else by the time she flies home? Visions of hip white lesbians with spiky hair and glittery chucks crowd my brain.[19] Maybe it would be easier for her if she was with a different girl, a girl better at being gay. I know Juniper has had her own insecurities with all my different sides. White and Asian. Femme and tomboy. Pansexual. Because of this I've always felt super insecure about the ways I didn't fit the type, didn't belong to the club. Just once I wish I could be one thing. But, alas. From birth I've always been one and two, this plus that.

After Juniper leaves, I take the weekend off from the letters to attend a poppy festival three hours away in Georgetown, a small town outside Austin, close to where Clark goes to college. A perfect little getaway to distract myself from Juniper's absence, how alone I feel. Baba's planning to visit his wife in Paris for the next

18 = date without her parents finding out = find a girlfriend.

19 = Ellen (both the pregnant teen and the talk-show host), Tegan or Sara, Rachel Maddow, Justin Bieber, for starters.

week, so I don't even have to come up with an excuse.

I briefly considered driving up to UT and surprising Clark. But things haven't been the same between us since he found out about Lola and Peter. A few days after Baba found out, Clark sat on the carpet in the middle of my bedroom, sighing one of those sighs that envelopes the entire room. As though his breath entered my body like a weight on my chest. "Do you understand I can't trust anyone? Not you, not Lola, not Baba, not Mom. I'm all alone." I wanted to scream back that this wasn't about him. This was about what had happened to Lola. That I was a kid, too. But, I knew he wouldn't listen. I wonder if he even knows that Lola's gone.

"Guāi-guāi,[20] lái le!" Baba screams from the kitchen loud enough to make the house quiver.

"Coming!" The hairs on my arms straight as soldiers. I worry his flight is canceled, or that something has happened, like his wife changed her mind. Who knew what was going on between them—he certainly didn't tell us. And I had too much going on to inquire.

To the refrigerator, he's taped a single white sheet of paper marked with a list of rules written in all caps in black marker:

1. DO NOT ANSWER DOOR TO ANYONE
2. DO NOT PUT POT IN MICROWAVE
3. DO NOT HAVE PARTY
4. DO NOT USE STOVE
5. KEEP DOOR LOCK
6. KEEP OUT OF GARAGE
7. WILL IN DRAWER IN STUDY

20 There's no perfect translation, but a thread on the r/AsianParentStories subreddit offers some insight. We've never been told what it means, but Baba always uses it as a term of endearment.

8. EMERGENCY MONEY IN SAFE (EMERGENCY ONLY!)
9. CONTACT NUMBERS IN DRAWER WITH WILL
10. NO PARTY!

I stare at the words inked on the page, how they bleed through the other side, trying to will myself to appear calm and collected, as though I wasn't planning to jump in my car the minute his Lyft drives out of sight.

"Oh, this just reminder for while you're gone?" I ask obediently, hands stuffed in my pockets.

Baba stares through me, then returns to the sheet of rules, jabbing it with his index finger. "Uh, yeah. Okay, so, uh, this just house rules while I out of town. Keep on refrigerator. Okay? I should be back in five days, so, not too long. If something happen to me, the will in the study, in the desk drawer." He runs his hand through his hair, checks his watch.

"Thanks, Baba! No problem. Have safe flight!"

Baba pats me twice on the head, then goes back to getting ready. I scamper back to my room and wait.

"Okay, see you!" Baba calls out as he closes the door behind him.

I stare at the car through my window facing the street as it takes off, watch it vigilantly until I'm sure I'm alone. I don't head to Georgetown until the United website confirms his flight has departed.

The first photo I post on Instagram after Juniper leaves is from the festival. I turn my phone on vibrate, slip it into my front pocket so I can hear it notify me if Juniper responds. I stroll through the parade, admire my namesake blossom all over the grassy medians as I try to imagine Juniper blooming, too, wherever she is.

golightlyintothatgoodnight

golightlyintothatgoodnight Everything's popping up poppies!

It's the first time since we've been together that Juniper and I have been apart. It's why Juniper urged me to take the weekend off from the letters.

"I know you, Poptart. The first couple days we're apart are gonna be hard for both of us, so I just don't want you to spin out from it all. That poppy festival sounds fun, and a great chance to take some photos. Please? I won't be able to focus unless I know you'll be okay. At least for the weekend. Okay?" Juniper asked while we were parked on the curb at the airport, her hand warming my cheek.

"Okay. Yeah, you're right. I think a break could do me good, give me some perspective. I can't believe we still haven't heard a peep from Lola, or from anyone else about where she might be." I sighed.

"I know. It's crazy. TBH, I think it's super fucked up that your parents aren't doing more to find her. I mean, I get it, they don't want to face what part they had to play in it all, but it's still fucked up. I hate that all of this is just landing on you. But, seriously. Just take a couple days off, okay?" Juniper's eyes darted to her phone to check the time.

"I know. It's kinda hard to believe they're not doing more to find her. But I guess I shouldn't be surprised. Don't worry about me, okay? I'll take the weekend to chill. Might as well take the opportunity to get out of the house while I can."

"Great! So relieved to hear that. Okay, Pops. Gotta jet. I miss you already! I'll text you as soon as I can." Her kiss tingled my cheek, and then just like that, gone.

Before Juniper took off, she Venmo'd me a little more money out of her savings so I could spend a couple of days in a cheap hotel. I check in to a room at an Airbnb just a ten-minute walk from the town square, where the poppy festival is being held.

A cup of coffee in hand, I stroll through the gardens close to the festival with a camera dangling from my shoulder. I snap a few photos of lily pads and daffodils the color of Pikachu, the dark shadow of my face looming over them in the frame.

On Sunday, I quickly gather my things into my duffel, click a quick shot with my phone for a future Insta post, and head towards home. The scarlet flash of poppies blurs into polka dots as I drive past. They cradle me, a reminder I have my own body outside of Lola's, my own story. I wonder if I'll ever be able to see myself outside of our twosome, a story that begins in some other way than "I am the one who tried to save my twin." I wonder how my own story would begin.

As I drive towards Galveston, last night's fight with Juniper plays over and over in my head. I try to tune it out by turning the speakers up on our playlist in the car, the one I made for her flight to Smith, but in this new light the songs just make my heart hurt.

By the time Juniper called last night, I wasn't in the mood to hear about how much fun she was having, how many cool queer girls she met, how perfect it would be if we could go there together. I couldn't tell her what I was really thinking. That I was afraid I'd never be able to escape Baba's clutches, not that far, for that long. Each word of frenzy and excitement she was experiencing away from me at Smith felt like a painful reminder of how far away she would be from me eventually, our fantasy of the last two years turning into nothing more than a dream I would wake from come fall. It was too much to bear.

I turned inward, grew quiet. I didn't mean to. I just didn't know how else to be.

"Poppy, what's wrong. Come onnnnnnn," Juniper sighed, annoyed. Defeated.

"Nothing! I'm just glad you're having such a great time. I'm happy for you." My lip quivered. I wiped the tears as they dropped on the receiver.

"Poppyyyyyyyyy! Please don't do this," Juniper implored, her tone tinged with resentment.

"Look. I get it if you want to hang up. I know I ruin everything."

I was bawling at that point, convinced I was just pushing her to hook up with someone by the time she got back, someone with less drama. I was just leading her to the inevitable conclusion I was too much to be with.

"Poppy. I love you, but you know I can't do this right now. I mean, this is a big deal for me. I thought you'd be happy I'm having fun here. I thought you'd want me to share this with you."

I blew my nose, took a breath. "I do. Honestly. But, I just don't understand why it took you so long to call." I could barely get out the words. I was sobbing full force now.

"Poppy! Come on. That's not fair. I have to focus while I'm here. I can't just be reassuring you all the time. Sometimes this all feels endless."

"What's that supposed to mean? I can't believe you would say that."

"Please don't do this. I'm begging you." I heard a cacophony of lilting voices call Juniper's name. She told them she'd be right there. "Look, I gotta go. I love you, okay? I'm not going anywhere, I promise. But please don't put this on us. I'll text you later."

I muffled the noise of my sobs into the pillow until I fell asleep.

We had to be ready for Baba's rage to sprout out of nowhere, like roots breaking through cement. I doubt even Baba knew when it would bubble inside of him. We had to be ready for Mom to suddenly decide she wanted us for a weekend or to plan a visit only to cancel it an hour after she promised to come. We had to be ready to wake up to strange men in Mom's house when we spent the night, beer bottles lining the bathtub, fruit flies circling the dishes in the kitchen sink. We had to be ready to wake up to the cloud of incense wafting from Mom's bedroom, lit to mask the scent of weed. We had to be ready for Mom to finally emerge in the middle of the afternoon, too tired and out of it to take us anywhere. We never had time to react, to resist the atmosphere as it morphed into a volcano, serene and magnificent and dormant one moment, ready to swallow us up the next. I learned I had to always be ready—to leave my heart somewhere else, and survive.

I began dating boys at sixteen, three years after Peter called Lola about the sleepover. At first, I was drawn to the havoc of teen boys. I wanted to live vicariously through the messiness of boyhood, the reckless entitlement. I quickly learned my ability to adapt didn't transfer to other parts of my life. I needed my life away from Lola and Baba and Mom to be steady, my body a boat aimed in a clear direction. I wanted love to be what I'd never gotten: simple, secure, and most of all, unthinking.

Usually, I didn't have to worry about that. Not with Juniper. She never let more than five minutes pass between texts. Juniper affirmed my doubts with texts as often as I'd need them, which, on a good day, was five to ten, but on a bad day could reach anywhere from thirty to fifty. She usually complied without judgment or frustration. Juniper knew it wasn't about her. She got it.

But, now, I find myself in foreign territory. I don't know how to adapt to her being gone. I've grown so accustomed to the texts, the Instagram dings, the Words with Friends back-and-forth, the spontaneous phone calls. I didn't realize how hard it would be once I couldn't count on them to be there.

I can't help it. I constantly pull my phone out of my pocket on my way to Galveston to check if she'll try to make up with me for the night before, or write back to the ten apology messages I sent long after she went to bed. I try to remember what she said before we hung up, her assurance that she still loved me even after I'd spun out, but my body feels suspended in the air, trying to find a way to land.

By the time I park by the beach, Juniper's tagged me in an Instagram post.

As soon as I click on Juniper's post, all the tension in my body just falls away.

juniperbutler
Northampton, Massachusetts

juniperbutler For my lover of tiny things.
You know who you are. #prettyinpink

July 28, 2019

Dear Twin,

When Peter asked you to spend the night with him, I didn't wait to hear your answer. I didn't want to know. I was too afraid.

I hung up the phone and ran to my room. But it didn't feel safe enough. So I hid in the bathroom with the door locked, fetal position on the cold linoleum. It was where I went when I thought I was in trouble and Baba was driving home to punish me. It was where I went that time I messed with the gold combination locks on his briefcase he used for meetings with new clients or theaters for Uzumaki Productions. I didn't mean any harm. I just wanted to pretend I was a businessman. I loved the way the coils felt against my skin as I moved them back and forth with my thumb, how the window light made them shine.

I should have known no locked bathroom would keep me safe. It didn't keep me safe from Baba's hand that day. And it wouldn't make what Peter said to you go away.

You must have heard the phone click

when I hung up. You tried to do damage control after you said whatever it was you said to him. I'm sure you knew when you looked at my face what I was most afraid of.

"Pops, you worry too much! He's a shūshu. He'd never do anything to us. Besides, I doubt it's even gonna happen. What would I say to Baba? I'm sure Talia will be there anyway. He is married, you know."

I went along with your story that day. But I just knew. Something was off. I could feel it in the bones we shared.

I heard the stories you told Baba when you thought I was in the shower and couldn't hear you. All-girl pool parties, sleepovers with friends we didn't have in common.

It would take time for me to get proof. When you could no longer bear keeping the secret to yourself. You were excited. Proud, you might say. You had to tell someone. Who else would understand but me?

That's when you showed me your diary. You showed me the entry of the day he came over to babysit while Baba and his wife were on a date. You and Peter sat on one sofa, I sat on the other. How he undid the round black buttons on the turquoise shirt we shared as I slept. The television played The Little Mermaid, our favorite. While Ariel tried to seduce the black-haired prince without words so she could win back her voice and have her happily-ever-after away from her controlling father, Baba's friend took you from me. And from yourself.

His mouth on your mouth.

His hand on your skin.

Our pair of turquoise shirts, no longer the same.

You told me not to worry. You promised me it hadn't gone farther than kissing. That he hadn't gone all the way. As if that would make it all okay. When it was clear I wasn't happy for you, you were mad. Disappointed your giggly confession didn't go as planned. You'll never admit it, but I'm sure you were dying to tell me he'd picked you over me. He'd chosen the better twin. I'm sure that made you feel good. Wanted.

I'm never sure if I'm saving you or putting you in more danger than anyone else. The first time I tried to save you I handed Baba your diary. The act of it felt like a punch in my gut, which was yours, too. We were thirteen. I didn't want it to get worse.

Baba set you up, so that he could save you. At least, that's the story

I told myself. He told Peter to come over one night, pretended we needed a babysitter. You didn't know. You were so excited. You thought you were in love. Like, what?

He was lying in wait. When Peter got out of his car parked on the street in front of our house, Baba threw his keys at him, threatened him to a fight.

Peter didn't say a single word.

He jumped in his car and took off.

That's when you told me you'd never trust me again. That looking at my face made you want to throw up.

Baba never spoke of Peter after. No one else did either - not the members of Uzumaki Productions or their children who we saw from time to time, not even his wife.

But. We felt what Peter had done hover over us like a curse. Baba picked apart the way you dressed, made you change if a shirt you wore showed a little belly, your dress sat too many inches too high on your thigh. I knew what he was insinuating, and I hated that for you.

It was the hardest thing I ever did, Lola. Tell Baba about Peter. If I had to do it again, I would. In a heartbeat.

Because if I had the chance to save

my twin, even if it meant she would never speak to me again, well, I would. A million times over I would.

I'm not saying I'm such a saint. I know it's selfish to want to save you.

I'm just saying that to me, that's what love is like. A person who loves you should try to save you from yourself even if there's a chance she'll never forgive you.

I just wish Baba would have seen it coming before it was too late. That was his job.

Love,
Poppy

11

This is what I was afraid of. One moment I'm standing on a cliff above a dark and unknown water I know could heal me if I could just be strong enough to dive, face first, into its mysteries and greater truths, and the next moment, I'm twisted and tangled in its murky, inscrutable depths, unsure of when or how my head will find its way above water and just how I will emerge, hopefully unscathed, reborn into a new self, one where the dirtiness of my past is sloughed off like snakeskin, washed away.

My body is my same body. My face is my same face. But my brain and heart and rumblings beneath the surface are no longer in my room, at my desk, at my typewriter. They're tumbling down an avalanche of memories.

I'm thirteen. I'm ten. I'm five. I'm sixteen. I'm twelve. I'm eight. The images of me in the various moments the letters conjure up for me move fast and all at once and thick and in blindingly bright shades like a Lynch remake of *The Wizard of Oz* in overexposed Technicolor. Terrorcolor, more like.

They're not all memories. Not exactly. My brain creates images, like movie stills, spliced from the myths I've been told by the other characters in our story. Like fear scenarios. My brain brings these to me in the form of nightmares while I sleep. Like that time in tenth grade when Baba's rage was at its peak and I lived in a constant state of panic he'd go off one day and never stop. And then there's the dream where I sit in a ghost chair in the middle of a wooden stage in an empty theater while Baba wedges a knife in my chest. There's no blood. I don't remember feeling any pain, but I recall staring mutely up at him, my face in a kind of numb shock, my mouth a soft circle of surprise, the kind that renders you voiceless. And then Clark enters from upstage. The face of the me in the dream lights up. Clark has come to my rescue! But Clark approaches Baba and says, flatly, "You're doing it all wrong," and twists the knife lodged into my chest. I wake up.

The whole day after the dream is a blur. Like a zombie, I float through the world that day riddled with shame of what my dreams portend, terrified that perhaps I've finally become unraveled, an outworn sweater. I wonder if I'm going crazy, completely unglued. How does one know when one's gone mad? All day long I'm unmoored by my brain's strange concoctions, panicking at what they signify.

There's also what Lola tells me about Peter, about Paolo. When those details suddenly alight in my imagination, I try to push them away. Each detail etched in the tenor of Lola's voice, almost indistinguishable from my own, paints me in shades of guilt, anger, sadness, fear. I try to get the memories of her telling me about them out of my head as soon as they arrive. But my will doesn't always overcome my brain.

July 29, 2019

Dear Twin,

(Just warning you, this one's gonna be a doozy.)

We were sixteen when Paolo started. You remember when we met this new friend of hers. Mom ate it up when Paolo and her Italian lovers, or those friends in between "Charmed" and "Can I buy you a drink?" wafted in and out of her apartment singing our praises as though they were being served to us off a conveyer belt. We didn't know it at first, but later we'd figure it out. That it was actually the two of us being served on a silver platter.

We loved the attention in the beginning, took to it like kittens lapping a saucer of milk. There were so many men that came through Mom's apartment that eventually we stopped remembering their names or asking how Mom met this one or that one. We stopped asking anything at all. We just smiled and nodded, giggled appropriately when this one or that one called us bookends, or precious, like porcelain China dolls. Even though we gave each other that tiny little look, the one that said we'd roll our eyes if no one would notice. The one that said with each poke of their dirty fingers, each twinned flattery, we shared the cringing we did inside. At some point the lilt of their individual accents all ran together, just like their faces. Besides, there was only one Italian man that mattered before Paolo. The one that started it all. Furio.

It's strange to know more about your mother's feelings for some Italian she met in Florence when you were six than even one sentiment she once held for your father. Furio never saw the dirtier parts of Mom. He never saw her flirt with every man at the club every night, and he never saw her temper thrash around in her body, once thin and frail and beautiful, now floppy and scattered and falling apart. He never saw her crumble at the reflection staring back at her from the full-length hallway mirror, the image she once knew of herself sewn onto the back of the image she now saw, an unattractive mess. He never saw her drink herself to normal, or the shot glasses lined along the rim of the bathtub, or the sink of neglected dishes, or how fucking often the world overwhelmed her.

I spent most of my life convinced it was only Baba that fucked up. I fell for Mom's trap, too. For a long time I did. That she was a victim because of all that had been done to her. She couldn't help catching pneumonia and getting fired. She couldn't help that her mom made her quit high school at fifteen to pay rent. It wasn't her fault Baba beat her or her own stepfather molested her. But it did seem like there was always someone to blame. If she always needed our allowance to pay for milk and eggs, even after getting food stamps, where did she get the money for weed and booze? What was Baba's child support going to? And what exactly was to blame for the fact that she was always leaving us?

She never stayed. She never left.

But, what can you do? She's Mom. How can you refuse her sympathy when you just want her like a swaddling blanket?

Let's face it. Even if Baba was perfect, we'd still need a mother's love. There's just that thing about mothers.

But, Furio. He was a bond she couldn't break. Traipsing all over Italy with some man she just met while Baba feeds us and clothes us and takes off work when we get chicken pox and makes the sandwiches for our sack lunches from fifty-cent packs of cold cuts at the grocery store. And scolds us when we get lice from Heather in daycare. And spanks us when we're too much, or ask for the wrong thing. Meanwhile, Mom's in Florence, meeting the love of her life. Another man who speaks a different language. Another man whose fractured English she can mock as though it's so cute when he gets an American expression wrong. But we know she does it to feel better about herself.

Mom and Furio love each other. They feed each other grapes off the vines of his cottage by the water and he reads her love poems in Italian while she stares lovingly into his green eyes and plays with his dark hair that so beautifully matches his skin. He proposes to her at sunset by the water. She starts to cry, imagining the new children she'll have in this new Italian romance. Maybe she'll have all sons, three strapping boys that will look just like the tall, dark, handsome stranger she sees before her. She's almost forgotten about those three children she had in the States once upon a time.

But. But. Then she remembers us. She

wants to fly us to Italy, have us meet her new love. It's his dealbreaker. He won't do kids. And that's that.

What if even that story isn't true? What if all those times she couldn't pick us up, even when it was her day to have us, what if she was just at home, and there's no Italy, no Furio, no romance? What does that make of us then?

Now she's in her forties. There's no Italian lover, no beautiful sons with muscles of oxen. Just three children from a marriage she wishes to forget and an exhausting life juggling waiting tables at the local hole-in-the-wall diner at night while selling medical equipment door to door during the day for a friend's business and picking up another friend's extra bartending shifts at the country club on some weekends. That diner becomes the closest she'll get to her Italian fantasy, except for those nights at the Italian Community Center in town where she flashes her brilliant blue marbles and white-toothed grin and brings another man home who she hopes will fall a little in love with her exotic, mixed-race twin girls, but not too much. Just maybe, he'll fall in love with them enough to love her, too. Secretly, she keeps hoping she'll find another Furio to take her away from the life she's in. It always looks more enticing on the other side of the ocean.

When you first told me about Paolo, I acted like it was normal. Like I was okay with it. I'd just come home from a date with a boy. You came into my room and asked me if I'd had sex with him yet. I was so innocent that I guffawed right there on the spot when you asked me, spit out a mouthful of Coke onto my worn jeans. You believed me.

"Okay, good. When you have sex for the first time, I want you to tell me," you said before leaving my room.

I nodded, my face hot from my own prudishness. It never occurred to me to ask why you wanted to know. My skin tingled in delight, I was so happy you cared. That I mattered.

It wasn't ten minutes later you came back. In your hand you held a crumpled-up piece of tissue. You were nervous, weighted. As if you held a secret.

It had been going on for months at that point. Paolo. Forty-three. Married. "This isn't like Peter," you said to me. This time, you were in love. I didn't point out that you swore you were in love last time, too. That his promises were interchangeable from Peter's three years before. Paolo insisted he was going to divorce his wife as soon as we graduated, and marry you. I knew he was your first. It was either him, or Peter. I could taste the acid at the back of my throat. I forced it down so you wouldn't know how horrified I was. And afraid. How disgusted I was with him. But most of all, that I couldn't believe this was happening all over again. Like a waking nightmare. If I only could slap myself awake.

I had never seen you feel bad about lying to me before - how could you expect me to tell you about losing my virginity if you'd already been on this journey without me, and hadn't even told me? I tried to act like I wasn't devastated you'd kept something this big from me for so long, tried to mirror the excitement I witnessed in your own version of our face, echo your own sound of our voice. The tissue was from the first time with him, and you kept it in your underwear drawer ever since as a souvenir. It made me shudder.

I knew I had to put a stop to it - who else would? - but I didn't know how.

I couldn't tell Mom or Baba or even Clark unless I was ready for what might happen. It would be two years before I had an opportunity to free you. When I had my moment, I didn't hesitate. Mostly because I couldn't take it anymore.

This is the part of the story you don't know yet. This is the part of the story that might make me lose you forever. But if we're going to come back together again, there can't be any more secrets.

Senior year. You were a secretary's aide. We both were. That's how you and Paolo found time to meet. You would key in an excused absence for yourself in the computer during our hour in the office when no one was paying attention, for a future date. On that date you'd walk into school with me as if everything was normal. When no one was looking, you'd sneak back outside to go a few blocks from school, where Paolo would be waiting. No one was ever the wiser. I went along with it, but I never told you how it ate me up inside.

Then, one day, just a few months before graduation, you messed up. You keyed in your absence, but after the secretary had already seen you so she knew it was a mistake. But what you didn't realize was she assumed it was just a typo. She called you to the office to double check. We were in the same Mandarin class. You sat in front of me, in the front row. When Chen Laoshi passed you the slip, you spun around to face me. Your eyes jittered.

"Shit. I fucked up on the computer. What should I do? Should I go to the office or just meet him now?"

I didn't want any part of this anymore. But I didn't know how to tell you that.

"Don't you think they'll get suspicious if you don't go to the office though?" I tried to seem nonchalant, logical. But I also hoped to keep you here, away from him.

You didn't listen. You texted Paolo to meet you, and then you were gone.

When the next slip that was handed to the teacher was for me, I didn't think anything of it. I thought it was just the secretary again, assuming I'd know what had happened since you didn't show up to the office.

But when I got there, it wasn't the secretary who wanted to see me. It was the principal. She wasn't alone. They'd called Baba out of concern when they realized you'd skipped school.

Baba asked me where you were, pretending he was a different kind of parent, one I could trust, one who didn't hurt me at the same time as he loved me.

"C'mon, guāi-guāi. Tell your Baba where she is. It's okay, we won't punish her. We just want make sure she safe."

Baba nodding and wearing a smile I'd never seen before. The principal smiling and nodding along with him.

"She's with Paolo," I managed to say to the person I feared most in the world. Our loving white-haired principal Mrs. Williams looking on, confused. She knew she didn't have the whole story.

"Who's Paolo?" she asked, although no one was listening to her. Baba knew who Paolo was because he was often at Mom's house when he dropped us off for the rare days she had custody and actually followed through with it. Sometimes Mom even had Paolo take us to Baba's house so she didn't have to get out of her pajamas.

Baba leaned towards me and stared at my face as though he could burn a hole through it with his dark eyes. I could tell what I said didn't compute. It kind of shocked me. It was like he'd totally forgotten about Peter, like what already happened didn't exist. It was like my words fell apart and floated in the air. I didn't want to repeat myself. It was hard enough to hear the words come out of my mouth the first time.

"She's. With. Paolo."

The second time I said it I was more deliberate. I paused between each word, emphasized each syllable like Baba was a child. I'd never spoken to him like that before. I would have been too afraid. But in that moment I was more afraid of what it meant for you to stay with Paolo, that every day Paolo got his hands on you, the more and more he could undo you. I did it for you. For me. For us. I did it for every girl that had a Paolo and parents who did nothing about it.

Baba shot up from his chair. Mrs. Williams tried to interject, tried to make sense of what was happening.

"I, uh, well. Paolo is my ex-wife friend. But. Lola has done something like this before, but last time with my friend. I need to call my wife. I need to call my friend, he's paralegal," Baba said out loud to no one.

Mrs. Williams slowly started putting it together. I knew she'd figured it out when she put a hand over her open mouth.

Baba kept muttering to himself, checking his watch, getting his phone out, putting it back in his pocket. For a minute I thought he forgot I was there. It wouldn't be the first time.

I remember trying to take up as little space as possible. It had taken everything in me to puff my chest out enough to say the words, and now that it was done, I deflated like a balloon.

"I mean. I know she adventurous, but why these men? Why our friends?"

He suddenly saw me then, my body squeaking in the cheap upholstery of the office chair, as I kept folding my feet underneath my knees until they slipped, and then did it again.

That's when he turned on me. That's when Baba became Baba again.

"How. Could. You. Not. Tell. Me."

It wasn't a question. He launched the words at me like barbs. I flinched, then burst into tears, covering my face with my hands. Mrs. Williams put a hand on my shoulder.

Then Baba told me not to tell anyone. That he would handle it. He asked me where you usually met Paolo. I told him. I could tell he was waiting to unleash the real punishment, for when we were all behind closed doors. I knew it was coming, but I didn't know what form it would take.

He rattled off question after question - when it started, and how often you saw each other. Where you went, for how long. I answered each question but I didn't know if each piece of information was going to protect you or only ensure that we would lose you forever. I didn't know which man would cause you more danger. I guess I'll never know.

Before he went back to work, Baba promised he wouldn't tell you that it was me that gave you up. He wanted to preserve our relationship. He patted me hard on the head, twice. And then he was gone.

That was the day that that cheerleader's boyfriend committed suicide after she wouldn't get back together with him. It was a strange sort of saving grace because she was in there with all her friends who were trying to comfort her. Honestly I just think they wanted to play hooky. I stayed in that chair all day, frozen in place. I didn't know if I was ever going to be able to leave the room.

But I had to leave eventually. It was opening night of Senior Musical - A West Side Story - and I was a chorus girl. For the last six months the musical was my main focus, but that day I couldn't imagine getting through it. The air around me just felt like a heavy cloak, now that the tragedy I'd been keeping from everyone for the last two years had been freed from its box. I had no idea what was going to unfold now that I'd let it out in the world. I was so afraid of going home. I was so afraid you would hate me forever.

I'm gonna stop there for now.

Love,
p

12

I wake up to the dried up tears from last night's letter, to thoughts of Paolo and Peter. I wake up afraid. I wonder if Lola's with Paolo now, if he kept his promise. Some mornings, Lola feels close enough to touch. Others, it feels as though galaxies separate us.

I try to set my mind right by daydreaming about Juniper, fantasizing about her in ways I usually don't allow myself while she's away—it would only make me long for her more than I already do. My phone snaps me out of my reverie.

> My little poppy seed muffin! I know you're probably sitting there thinking about us in your wondrous koala ways and about all the blah stuff with the evil twin and grossness of the past, but I want you to stop all that right now. And listen to this song. Like, RIGHT NOW. It's like YOUR life, literally, except for the best line, the one that made me think of you to begin with. You'll know which one. I am here to tell you that you ARE gonna make it, and it's not gonna kill you. You're gonna get through this, and you're gonna be better than ever after you get all of it out of you. Because you are the strongest, most resilient popcorn I know. And because I know you're never gonna let the world you came from dictate the world you will become part of, which is now, which is tomorrow, which is forever. I love you so much, and I can't wait to tell you every single detail of what it's like here. I

> can just picture us here so much it hurts because I just want us to be here right now! I couldn't have been the panda you know and love if I didn't know I had you to come home to, to Insta, to text, to make fun of posers with, and to watch you put on a fashion show for me in just two days! Just you wait. It's gonna be on. And I'm gonna attack the shit out of you with so many cuddles and so many smooches . I miss and need my good luck charm so so bad. <33333 xoxo

I sing Juniper love songs. Songs everyone else thinks are universal but we know are meant only for us. We fall into the words I sing in front of my phone as the voice memo app charts the rise and fall of my pitch like an EKG. Like scanning our hearts.

But, Juniper. Juniper sends me videos of songs. She's too shy to sing any song she loves, any song she wants to share because she never feels deserving of the song. And besides, typically the band and the singer make what Juniper feels is the most perfect kind of song in and of itself. She can't bear to jinx its magic by acting as though she can do it better justice. She sends music videos that say something about how Juniper is with me, or some feeling she has for me expressed more eloquently by Karen O or Tilly and the Wall or Perfume Genius or CHVRCHES or Phoebe Bridgers or Haim or Kishi Bashi or Sigur Ros or Iron & Wine or Sufjan Stevens or Janelle Monáe or Mitski or Japanese Breakfast or Hayley Kiyoko or BTS or or or or or or or. Or The Mountain Goats, who Juniper captions our story with this morning, or rather, my story, this time. It's one of the most loving things Juniper does, texting me her understanding of my story and the way her brain writes that story through a song she has loved for so long, and I know her texting this song to me is her way of letting go of the tight clutch of that song between her grasping fingers.

It's as if Juniper is saying: "This is how much I love you. I know this song will help you understand yourself better, so go, go be with this moment of words against sound and let it fall over you like magic pixie dust and let it remake you. It will give a name to the sadness, and then it will let you move from that sadness into a new body, one that knows of sadness but doesn't suspend itself inside of it." I never tell Juniper this, but I live for these moments, never pushing for them. I know they'll come when I need them the most.

I have a process for how I listen to the songs Juniper sends me. First, I listen to the song as it comes to me, watching the video and grabbing words and phrases like droplets of rain. Then I open Spotify, search for the song, minimize the app on my phone. Then I find the Genius page online, and finally I read the lyrics as I listen. Sometimes I'm compelled to record myself singing the song and send that recording back to Juniper as if to say: "Here. This is what my heart sounds like mouthing the words you gave to me. Can you hear the little pulsing creature inside rewriting my story through the words? This is what I sound like changed by the gems you let out of your box for me to adore and treasure."

This is what I find when I pull up the song Juniper sends me this morning:

I broke free on a Saturday morning
I put the pedal to the floor
Headed north on Mills Avenue
And listened to the engine roar

My broken house behind me
And good things ahead
A girl named Cathy

Wants a little of my time
Six cylinders underneath the hood
Crashing and kicking
Aha! Listen to the engine whine

I am going to make it through this year if it kills me
I am going to make it through this year if it kills me

I played video games in a drunken haze
I was seventeen years young
Hurt my knuckles punching the machines
The taste of Scotch rich on my tongue

And then Cathy showed up
And we hung out
Trading swigs from a bottle
All bitter and clean
Locking eyes
Holding hands
Twin high maintenance machines

I am going to make it through this year if it kills me
I am going to make it through this year if it kills me

I drove home in the California dusk
I could feel the alcohol inside of me hum
Pictured the look on my stepfather's face
Ready for the bad things to come

I downshifted as I pulled into the driveway
The motor screaming out stuck in second gear
The scene ends badly as you might imagine

In a cavalcade of anger and fear

There will be feasting and dancing in Jerusalem next year

I am going to make it through this year if it kills me
I am going to make it through this year if it kills me

I know Juniper knows, about Baba's rage and violent temper, about Clark hiding his wounds inside his video games and food. Juniper knows how each year is about surviving a moment at a time until that moment becomes a day and a week and a month and a year. Juniper knows how many of the scenes of my life I was just waiting for the bad things to come and the look on Baba's face and the cavalcade of anger and fear and seventeen years young and the crashing and the kicking and the broken house from behind and the good things ahead.

Because Juniper pays attention. Because she loves me enough to. When I read the lyrics and listen to the song, I hear not just the song and not just the point of Juniper sending it but I also hear Juniper's attentiveness to my entire self, not just the part of me that loves and giggles and coos and yelps, but also the bad parts, the fear and anger and shame and sadness and trauma and abuse, the parts hardest to hold. Each happening grows inside of me like a body with a stronger and stronger heartbeat and the other body inside, the bad one, the wounded one, has a heartbeat, too, but one that grows softer and softer as the first grows stronger. With each letter to Lola, with each love note from Juniper, the bad one is dying out. As the song comes to a close, I begin to wonder, is the love from Juniper and the resolve for the kind of life I am determined to have in the end—one wide awake and whole and, if at all possible, healed—fiercer and bigger than the worst part of the Lola story?

I know what I have to do. I have to finish the letters. I have to get the story out of me and onto the page for Lola to do with as she will. So that I can be free. It's as though I've entered the world in an already-built cage and with each letter I write, each foot planted into a new life with Juniper, each bar on the cage begins to fade. Each letter removes a bar of my captivity. Each moment with Juniper adds a brick onto the house I will build of my new life. I could embody what the song tells me, what Juniper means to tell me—that I can do it. I can leave my broken house behind me, and move on to good things ahead.

July 30, 2019

Dear Twin,

You know all this, but let me get it out.

Baba, who I'd never seen drink a beer, chain-smoking in his room nonstop. His wife had been part of our life since we were ten, and gradually she'd begun to care for us in ways that were maybe beyond her role, but she could see that we didn't have a mother who could be there for us in the way that we needed. She tried to help in her own way, tried to intervene when Baba let himself get carried away. But that was before. I don't blame her for leaving when it all went down. She didn't know what to do with the unraveling man before her. So, she fled to Paris to stay with a friend. Who knows if she'll ever come back.

Mom filed charges against Paolo, for indecency with a minor. No one wanted to admit what they'd let happen - that it was much worse than that. She kept asking me if you'd slept with him before you turned eighteen. I told her yes. Again and again, when she would corner me in the dark hallways of her small apartment while you were in the bathroom. She wouldn't listen. She didn't want to hear what her obsession with Furio had caused.

Clark never forgave me for not coming to him about this. I'm not sure what he would have been able to do, but he, too, came to my room in the pitch black one night while you were asleep.

"I can't believe no one told me this. I can't believe you didn't tell me. My entire family has lied to me." His face distorted in the dark, cut by betrayal and rage.

I tried to tell him that wasn't what mattered. What mattered was we needed to help you.

"No one told her to jump on top of these men. No one told her to dress like that, to flirt with Peter and Paolo. If it's not her fault, why didn't it happen to you?"

I haven't spoken to him since he said that to me. I think the feeling is mutual. He won't forgive me for not telling him what was happening with Paolo, and I'll never forgive him for blaming you for what they did.

And then, there's what Baba said to you.

"How could you do this to me?"

"If I go crazy and kill him and go to

jail, will you feel responsible?"

"Why can't you find boys your age? Why do you have to take my friend, your mom's friend?"

"You know Paolo married, right? You know he has family? You know you can go jail for skipping schools?"

"I can't believe how much pain you cause me. Tǎo yàn."

What I was most afraid of didn't happen. He didn't lay a hand on you. He didn't "go crazy and kill him," but he always held you responsible for what their bodies did to yours. After Mom filed charges against Paolo, he went back to the police station and filed an inactive police report against Peter. But, because you refused to testify that you were a minor, Baba claimed there was nothing more he could do. After Mom filed charges, the courts set you up with a therapist. But all that therapist did was ask about Baba. You barely told the therapist anything of use. And so after you did the required five sessions, that was that.

I'd hear Baba's wife say to one of her friends on the phone, an American friend so I could understand enough to eavesdrop, that if you and Paolo were in love, what could they have done to stop it?

But, I don't know, why didn't anyone say that what Peter and Paolo did was wrong? Why didn't they ask you what happened? Why didn't they talk to us about what it meant when older men think they get to take young girls' bodies? What did they say in what they didn't say?

Love,
p

13

In the dream, we're living in Northampton. Our life in the dream is also a dream I don't want to ever wake up from.

Juniper doesn't expect me home for a few hours yet. I pick up a dozen calla lilies—her favorite. Today it's my turn to have the car—we left my Corolla when we fled from home a few weeks before the semester started. Two cars were too much to negotiate.

I want to surprise her.

I park the car in the driveway of our rental house, juggle the backpack that dangles from one strap off my left shoulder, hold the huge glass vase of lilies in my arms. I can't wait to see the look of delight spread across her face, can't wait for the kisses she'll drop all over my cheeks.

I hear murmurs, the noises of bodies smacking against one another. My heart lurches in my throat.

It's like a bad movie, coming home early to surprise Juniper only to find her in the act of betrayal.

When I get to the bedroom, though, it turns into a horror film.

Lola's mouth on my Juniper, Lola's legs curved around my love's waist. The vase drops from my arms, shatters everywhere. I stand in a puddle of water, surrounded by shards of glass. My face is pockmarked red, transparent splinters wedged in my skin instead of the kisses I'd imagined would be in their place only moments before.

"Poppy!" Juniper's mouth an O of confusion. "I thought she was you."

July 30, 2019

Dear Twin,

Where are you? Sometimes, like when I woke up this morning, I get the feeling you're close by, but I wish I knew where. I know we always talk about what bullshit ESP is, especially the way they talk about it on TV. Like that Unsolved Mysteries episode we watched where a twin goes into labor in the back of a van and her identical twin feels all her labor pains while lying in her bed trying to sleep. But even still, I keep getting the uncanny feeling that you're just around the corner. I hope I'm right.

Remember when Patrick in seventh grade would hit one of us, and then ask the other "do you feel that?" Or when Jason, who was such an idiot, asked "do you have the same number of hairs, ahem, down there?" God. Boys are so ughs.

I used to hate the stories Mom told us about how twinny we were, but ever since you've been gone, I can't help but play those stories again and again in my mind. They make me feel closer to you, even when you feel achingly far away. It comforts me to think there's this thread between us, no matter how fucked up and hard it is to be your twin. I wish I hadn't taken it for granted that you'd always be there.

When we got our booster shots and we only cried during each other's.

When you started walking first, but then you saw I wasn't walking and so you sat your bottom right back down on the living-room carpet and refused to take another step until I did.

When we shared the same crib and Mom was scared something was wrong because we didn't make a peep.

When Mom said as toddlers we watched Clark wreak havoc around the house like spectators at a tennis match - our heads turning back and forth, just following him with our eyes without a sound.

Those little moments where we said the same thing at the same time without even trying.

Those days we'd dress alone in our rooms and come out wearing the same thing (I wish you didn't always make me change, that made me sad).

Watching movies with Clark and Baba and when we thought something was cute, we'd turn to each other, smiling a little smile, and then turn our faces back to the television set. How it freaked everyone else out that whatever it was that transpired between us didn't need to be spoken out loud.

That time Mom made us go with her to the Freedom Festival downtown for the Fourth of July and then she got drunk and started sliding on the huge hills that had turned into mud after it started to downpour. And we hid under Mom's broken umbrella, our arms shivering the same. We were cold, but we had each other to keep us warm.

All the songs we would sing together - all the Disney ones of course, and sometimes Phil Collins, and Sam Cooke, and Cher, and Madonna, and the Four Tops. You humored me with Sam Cooke, so I humored you with Cher. Back when compromises were easy. When everything was easy. Like when I gave you all my potato chips, and you gave me all your cookies.

That Christmas when Mom couldn't afford a tree so she had us do what she did with her Montessori babies she was teaching then. Trace our hands on construction paper of all the colors and cut them out and tape them to the wall. How we'd point and laugh when we fucked one of them up - you missed a

finger, or I lost control of my pen and
it just looked like a big green blob.

Remember when it was like that all
the time between us? All the laughs,
all the colors? I wish we could go
back there, before Paolo and Peter and
everything else got in the way. Before
they turned everything gray.

I hope you really haven't totally
gone away yet. I hope it's because
there's still time to bring us back, to
the way we used to be.

Please come home.

Love,
p

14

Lola and I weren't the only ones damaged by Baba. It's something I don't like thinking about too much, because what had happened to Lola was more than enough to deal with. When it came to Lola, I felt I had a role to play. Which means I felt I could do something about it. I guess I wanted to believe there was something I could do to unmake what had been made.

"Help your sister, and I know you will," Baba would say.

"You're her sister. You need to make sure she doesn't go astray, like I did," Mom would say.

When Mom would tell us the story about how Baba said, if she tried to fight for full custody, "I burn the house down with everybody inside," I knew she could never protect us. How could she just leave us with him after he threatened our lives? How could a man that threatened our lives ever truly keep us safe?

Lola wasn't the same after Peter and Paolo. She saw herself as grown up in a way I wasn't. No longer a girl, but a woman who was wanted by men. But that wasn't all. She saw me as the one that came between her and love. Her eyes, which used to look at me with laughter and knowing, now were cold and empty. She reserved those feelings for someone else instead. I was the one that got between her and what she wanted, who she felt wanted her. So she punished me. With little jabs, but most of all, with her absence. And when Lola gradually began to vanish, I was the one Baba scolded in her place.

"You know, guāi-guāi, I won't be around all the days. I wish sometime you help her understand her behavior. I mean, you see her with these mens, why you do nothing? How come you stay home and well-behave and she like this? That's what sisters should do. Look out for each other. You know she won't listen to me."

Of course, Baba doesn't know about my relationships with boys, and he definitely doesn't know about Juniper. I'm the invisible one. Baba never asks why he never sees me with anyone, or why I spend such long hours out of the house. He barely says a word to me. Maybe he doesn't want to know. Lola's enough to handle.

But, it's not just the two of us. There was Clark. Each Uzumaki child suffers. I'm the invisible savior, the placeholder, the fixer. Lola's the Lolita, just as she'd been cast from birth, the keeper of the family secret, the nymphet to become prey. As for Clark, well, Clark had the marrow sucked out of his bones the way a boy so often does.

With Baba, I'd always been afraid. And although he'd struck us, on occasion, it wasn't his hand that most filled me with fear. It was the threat of violence and of being sexualized by the men he subjected us to that caused the greatest terror and agony. In a way, the threat was worse than the happening. It was the imagining of the almost happening that horrified me most, what I envisioned in my mind was always, always, always worse than the outcome. That was the thing with outcomes: they happened, and then, they were over. They might change your life forever, they might try to take your spirit, but it's somehow easier to deal with than all the different ways your brain could concoct scenarios of what-ifs, building them like walls of bricks. What burned itself into my brain was the demonic look in his eye when he asked me to kill him as he struck his own face again and again in front of me in my bedroom in the dark, the moon reflected against the window my only witness. "Do you want to slit my wrist [SLAP], cut my throat [SLAP], suck my blood [SLAP]?" I'd never forget the dark shriek he pitched at my face.

Clark's different. As an Asian father, Baba was expected to discipline his son. That's how you turn him into a man. You hit not necessarily because you want to but because it's the only thing that will teach him respect. Baba's the mother who cooked and kept a house and Baba's the father who disciplined his son. Baba's son became sullen and lethargic because that's what he did to deal with being in a house like that. But to Baba, he was lazy and undisciplined. When his son got reprimanded at school for terrible handwriting or drawing comics when he was supposed to study, or got an 82 in English class instead of the highest score, Baba snapped. And when he snapped, it was a shotgun going off in the night, choked in silence.

"You see all these award on the wall?" Baba would point at the wall of plaques in the study, awards he'd won for his carpentry and his contributions to Uzumaki Productions. "Many people respect me. You have a lot to learn from me before you leave this house. You think you big shit, walk around, so lazy. You nothing. Nothing!"

Struggles always ensued. Baba always won. Clark became smaller, quieter. Less.

Baba didn't know any better. He didn't get that the beatings made it worse. That screaming until his voice turned to a squeak and rubbing Clark's mouth with soap made it worse. That shoving Clark's face into the dirt that fell on the car floor mat, from a cup that held a seed tucked into soil Clark had been given to take home from school to watch grow into a vine, and slashing Clark's young beige skin with hundreds of words broke his son down until Clark could no longer become the man Baba felt it was his responsibility to make him into. Baba never recovered from losing Clark. Neither will Clark.

Clark didn't disappear like Lola. He's still at UT. He still has pretty girlfriends, ones Baba can be proud of. Clark lives an appropriate life. But, everyone knows that Baba beat Clark's spirit into white dust as it fled his body. Everybody knows Clark will never be the same. Baba just doesn't get it. Baba sees Clark as proof of his failure as a father because Clark doesn't attend Harvard and he makes strange, illogical decisions and he parties too much (although, compared to the average white boy, he doesn't party nearly enough), and he doesn't study as much as he should. But, this is not the reason Baba failed Clark. The reason Baba failed Clark still lingers in the dirt on that floor mat that has since been vacuumed away.

But. Clark made living in the Uzumaki house tolerable. We had a bond that not even Lola and I have. Clark could paint and draw like no one I'd ever seen. He could sculpt. In high school, Clark had this huge glitter nail-polish collection, bigger than anyone else in school, and he would paint these delicate figures on our fingernails when we went to dances, and for all of his friends who were girls, too. Even for Vaughan, this Black gay boy I met in theater class who was my favorite person (besides Juniper) before he moved back to Atlanta with his dad. Surprisingly, his nail-polish hobby is completely accepted within the fabric of the family. Even Baba's wife would buy Clark manicure sets for Christmas, or a bottle of pink glitter.

It was more than just our being artists that connected us. Clark got it. He got the sadness we had been born from. And he, too, had a desire to break free. Just before he stopped coming home, we began to share music, too. I loved Motown, the low crooning of the men's voices supported by the dancing backbeat. For Clark, it was rap and hip hop, and soon he was making beats and writing down lyrics instead of painting or inking the panels of his comic books. Motown inspired me to read the great Black American writers: Baldwin, Ellison, Lorde, Hurston, Brooks, Wright. Soon I began to connect my story with Baba as one tied to double consciousness.[21]

I never felt at home in Baba's Asian world, and felt mostly out of place among the white kids that dominated the halls (and the world). I knew how it felt to be constantly at odds, constantly judging yourself by how you are seen, instead of by how you see yourself.

21 W. E. B. Du Bois.

July 30, 2019

Dear Twin,

The other day I was watching Great Balls of Fire! We were so into that movie. It's kinda fucked if you really think about it. And it was ALWAYS on cable. How old we were when we saw it for the first time? Was it before we were thirteen? Sometimes I wonder if it had anything to do with what happened with Peter. This famous singer falling for his thirteen-year-old cousin. Making her a dollhouse. Tickling her. It's kind of gross how young she feels in the film, like a child. The way she twirls her bubble gum around her finger, batting her big blinky eyes while she swishes her poodle skirt. Everything he does is so vulgar in comparison. I guess that's the point.

Can a movie have that much power?

It's scary to think about.

Love,
p

15

In two days, Juniper will be home.

I finish washing my face and brushing my teeth, trying to decide if I'll write another letter today, or take another breather. I just emailed Juniper to tell her a new idea I had for the letters, of compiling them into an autobiographical young adult novel:

> What d'ya think? I could turn this whole thing into a book. I know, Capricorn probs. But still! I could call it *Letters to Lola* (or a fake name I come up with) and I'd fictionalize the letters to protect our privacy (and her story) but it could be a young adult novel ACTUALLY WRITTEN BY A TEEN and like, I don't know, a way for other teens to witness what it feels like to be in the trenches of stories like these that don't get told. The book could be for the people that never get written about. The Poppys and the Lolas, and even the Junipers.) I miss you so much! Write soon please!

My phone rings, playing a ringtone of Janelle's "Make Me Feel," since it was the first song we ever danced to. We were at a lesbian night at an 18+ club. Every time my phone rings, I'm right back in that darkly lit bar, surrounded by a glorious scene I once never knew existed: young hipster genderqueers in T-shirts and chucks, Latinx femmes in red lipstick and floral skirts, Black butch women swaying with their plus ones. Juniper sways her body in front of mine until we both get the courage to shrink the space between us, her denim-wrapped thigh catching my stockinged calf as we twist and fold and find our way to a groove together. I shiver. Now when the song plays on the radio, Juniper makes karaoke faces accompanied by her signature dance move, which involves crouching low and pretending to swish her flat booty back and forth while pumping both her fists in the air. Sometimes she'll grab me and jerk us back and forth super fast and then giggle so hard tears squeeze out of her closed eyelids. I laugh so much I can't possibly dance along because Juniper is far too entertaining. I like knowing the minute my phone sings when it's Juniper. Our ringtone is like most everything else between us. Even when it's popular, it's important in the most idiosyncratic ways no one on earth would understand but the two of us.

My heart pirouettes awake at the sound of it. I always wait to answer it until the second ring because the song makes me giggle and dance along in spite of myself before I remember, *seriously, pick up the phone already!*

"Junebug!!!!!!!" I whispersqueal as I hold the phone very close to my mouth.

"Hi cute little pop rocks!" Juniper yips back.

"How come you're calling???!!!"

"Oh, cause I wanted to hear your voicccccce. It's been out of control over here and so I didn't get to write back to your amazing little email. So I just thought I'd, you know, pick up the phone and hear the cute little Pops being all Pops-like."

"Aw, that means a lot. So ... what did you think?!"

"Dude. Amazing. Like, so meta, and you know how I love that meta shit. But, maybe you can call it *Letters to My Twin* and name her Ada, like that creepy book by Nabokov. Right? And it has that whole twin thing in it already."

"Oh my god. Genius. So good. YES!"

"Awwww, my cute little Pops. I miss you. But yes, I love it and I can't wait to see you so you can tell me all about it in that cute excitable little Pops-a-lot way."

I'm so thrown off by the call that I almost forget to ask about her trip. I never want to be the kind of girl who doesn't ask about her girlfriend's life. Ever.

"So tell me, we haven't even talked about your lesbian adventch!"

Juniper pauses.

"Uh, yeah, I was wondering if you were gonna bring it up! It's amazing, but also wild to be around so many queer folk. I can't wait to take you here. But also, like, SO MANY GRANOLA WHITIES."

"June! You are incorrigible."

"What do you mean? It's not my fault they don't have the panache of gaysians. UGH. Speaking of. I gots to go do one more thing today before I pack and you know how packing drives me bonkers. I just wanted to hear your voice for a second, little Popchip. I'll see you so soon though! Love you!"

"Love you! I can't wait to see you!"

We say bye four or five more times. As I hang up the phone, I realize there's something I need to do, too.

July 31, 2019

Dear Twin,

Paolo went to jail for a month. We found out later his wife was pregnant - and that the stress of what happened caused her to miscarry. She sent you hate mail, nicking at your spirit even further by calling you a whore. I wanted to burn the letter, but you insisted on keeping it. That never made any sense to me.

I knew exactly when he would be released. I felt it was my job to know, my job to protect you.

When we went to court, a psychiatrist took the stand and said that she'd given him a thorough evaluation, and that her findings led her to conclude he was a pedophile. Your scream rang out into the courtroom. You refused to testify against him, refused to believe it was true. That you were one of many. Who knows what girls had been at his mercy before Mom brought him into our life? We'll never know.

If you had tears, you hid them from me. But I could feel your sadness in the short distance between our rooms and our bodies. I didn't know what to do about it.

Just a month after we sat in that courtroom and watched him walk away in handcuffs, he called. It was the second day of summer break, maybe ten in the morning. He must have known Baba wasn't going to be home. I don't know how, since he spent so many days in the garage working. But on this day, Baba had gone to a meeting. Somehow he'd gotten a hold of Baba's landline. I wonder if it was through you.

I answered.

The person on the other end of the phone spoke in a low, muffled, and strange voice. Like they were calling from underground. I knew it was him. I felt it in my skin. I wish you had still been asleep. I wish you had gone to the bathroom. I wish you had been downstairs getting a snack.

All the wishes stack up, they're too much to bear.

You heard your name through the phone. You grabbed the phone from my hand with a kind of aggressive enthusiasm.

I can't remember what story you told me about who it was on the phone. But, I knew. Because I know you. I saw you jut your chin out, reveal your neck the way you always did when it was about a boy. I saw your eyes light up. I knew this wasn't about a boy. I knew this was about a man, the man who got away, the man I had hoped would stay there.

Hours later, after Baba had come home after his meeting to make lunch for us before he headed back out to meet a potential client, the Texan sun beat hard through the blinds. You ran out, said you were going for a walk. You hated the heat. It made no sense. I was in the bathroom when you left, and as I heard the door click behind you, my heart dropped to my feet. I was convinced you were gone. Forever. And I knew it was Paolo that you had gone to.

I finished peeing, not even waiting to flush the toilet. I threw my sandals on and ran down the block after you, even though I had no idea what direction you took. You were nowhere in sight.

The streets and the sidewalks were empty. Empty of passersby. Empty of you and Paolo. We were eighteen now. What could I do?

I screamed. Then I flung my head onto my thighs and fell against the pavement and began to sob.

I stood up, and began to walk back to the house, dejected, my feet dragging on the sweltering concrete.

Just as I turned the corner to go back into the house, I heard the sound of feet, thump thump, coming towards me. There you were. Your bare feet smack-smack-smacking against the sidewalk. How could you stand the burning cement?

"I called and called and called you! Didn't you see me?!" you snapped. We both knew it was bullshit. But I went along with your story because I was scared any resistance would mean you would go away from me again. That Baba and Mom wouldn't recover. And they'd blame me for it. I didn't know, even after everything, how to live without you.

"Where were you?" I managed to ask, because I couldn't help myself.

"Oh, I was just sitting by the pool, getting a suntan."

I'd checked the pool. Every inch of it. You weren't there. But I didn't say that.

Later, I'd find out that Paolo had parked on a nearby street, in a Lincoln Town Car with tinted windows. Kissed you. Told you that he hadn't said he was in love with you before because he knew it would have fucked both of you up. But then, he decided to tell you anyway.

At least, that's what you told me happened.

Now, I'm just hoping this wasn't a plan all along - that graduation marked your freedom, and now he could take you away without consequence or remorse.

But I guess remorse isn't something he ever had.

I don't have any more left in me to write. Maybe another day.

Love,
p

16

Baba beats me to it.

I haven't been home long—I'd told Baba I'd gone to the library to study. I was planning to send the most recent letters to Lola, but I'd forgotten them in my rush out the door. Baba's still in the garage when I get home, and I don't think much of it.

I take off my shoes, put them in the shoe closet. I run up the stairs, use the bathroom.

Before I leave the bathroom, I hear it. The back door slamming closed—crack—like a rocket going off in the middle of the night. And I know something's happened. But, I've been here before. Whatever set him off this time could be anything. I know better than to try to guess.

"Guò lái !" Baba yells from the kitchen. I've become an expert at knowing where exactly he is depending on how far his voice carries.

Everything inside me suspends in time, space. I remind myself to breathe in and out. I wish Lola was here.

"Coming!" I yell back, trying to pretend nothing's wrong, trying to pretend my body isn't shutting down from fear.

Nothing could prepare for me for what I see in the kitchen.

Baba's heavy breath sucks up all the air in the room. Baba's sweaty hand, holding a letter.

My letter. To Lola.

And I can tell from his darting look he's opened it. He's read it.

As I wait for him to let me have it, I sift through my memories as quickly as possible. I can't remember if Baba knows Paolo ever came here. I try to search the file in my mind for that moment, but it's blank. Where I want an answer, there is only emptiness.

"So. Tell me. How long you been doing this? Writing these letters?" He waves it at my face. I'm cloaked in his heavy breathing, the sweat dripping from his hair down his face until it slips under his black tank top, his one hand pressed against his hip, his other hand gripping my words meant only for her. Why didn't I keep these letters in a locked box hidden in the depths of my closet? Why did I ever trust that anything of mine would ever be safe? What on earth was I thinking?

"Uh. I don't know. Not that long," I manage to say back to him, my words so tiny next to his. This is a dynamic we're both familiar with.

"She write back?" Something is different this time. I have something he wants. And then I remember. This isn't only his conversation. This is mine, too. Lola is mine, too. More mine than his.

"No."

"Okay, okay. You tell me if she write back, okay?"

This can't be the end of the conversation, can it? When will the other shoe drop?

But the rage doesn't come. At least, not from him.

"No, Baba. Not okay." I want to throw up. But I have to do this. It's my only chance, and I'm going to take it. For her. For us.

"Wait. What? What you say to me?" I can see the blood bubble in that one vein in his forehead that always twitches when he gets angry. I finger my phone in my jean pocket. I can always call the police if he goes off the deep end, and then make a run for it.

"It's not okay that you haven't reported her missing. Or driven the entire length of Houston to find her. She's been gone all summer. Don't you even care? Or do you only care about your show, your furniture? I know you're making your next show about her. I'm not stupid."

"You listen to your Baba. If you going to live in my house, girl, you better—"

"I better what? Respect you? She's gone! She could be anywhere. She could be with Paolo, or Peter. Or worse. Do you know what would happen if they got a hold of her forever? Mom's gone. Why won't anyone do anything about this?"

I start to cry. I can't stop.

Baba's not sure what to do. He awkwardly pats me on the shoulder. "Uh, I just don't know. She eighteen, she's legally adult. What can I do? Beside, if they in love, then—"

"They CAN'T be in love, Baba! He's YOUR age. She's a teenager! What the fuck."

"If you so worried about her, why didn't you protect her? You her sister. You supposed to keep her out of trouble."

That's all it takes to know it's no use. I wipe my face, snatch the letter out of Baba's hands. I grab my keys and walk out the door.

Baba is yelling for me, but he can't help me now. As I back out of the driveway, I can still see him through the kitchen window. He's stopped yelling after me. His hands hang by his sides, limp. And for once, I don't feel anything except pity.

July 31, 2019

Dear Lola,

The other day I read an essay that was shared on Twitter about the real Lolita. Your namesake. There's this book by Sarah Weinman called The Real Lolita: The Kidnapping of Sally Horner and the Novel that Scandalized the World. In the book, the author "investigates the 1948 case of Horner, who was abducted as a child by the con-artist and pedofile, Frank La Salle. Horner lived with La Salle as his captive for two years, spending her 12th and 13th birthdays on the road as he took her from her New Jersey hometown across the US to California. Horner's story is also Dolores Haze's story. Through careful critical investigation, Weinman maps out how Nabokov learned of, and developed Lolita around, reports of Horner's kidnapping and abuse."[22]

I never did know how to feel about Lolita. It seemed like a curse to name you after the most famous story of

22 "The Lasting Effects of the Lolita Complex," Lacy Warner.

pedophilia in all of classic literature. For the most part, all Lolita did was to remind me how Mom couldn't even name you right. Names are powerful, and we inherit what's behind them. I truly believe that. But now that I know there's a real girl behind that story, a girl that was abused and broken by a real man, I can't untie the knots my stomach makes to reckon with it. You were a real baby girl too. You deserved to be given a name of strength.

I haven't read the book, but based on the essay, the writer says that the girl called her brother-in-law and finally escaped La Salle's clutches. But, two years after she was kidnapped, she died in a fatal car accident. Her whole life culled down to a single note, a note of her being stolen rather than a note of her simply being, defined on her own terms.

I don't know where you are, but I hope that doesn't become your story. It's that ending I'm most afraid of.

Remember when we were kids, and Baba drove us to Chinatown and I was chewing bubblegum? You were lying on your stomach in the back seat - it was Clark's turn to sit shotgun - and I started braiding your hair. You hardly ever let me touch your hair, so I was really getting into it. Smacking my gum and playing with your hair. We were giggling, you were unusually relaxed. And then I found a huge knot in your hair and I let my mouth drop open without realizing it, as I tried to figure out how to untangle it without making it hurt too much. I forgot about the gum. It fell out of my mouth and landed in your hair. I cursed, and tried to take it back. But it was too late. Baba had to cut it out. My punishment was that he cut the same amount of hair out of my head, too.

I still think about that day, the cutting. I wish I could cut these men out of you just like Baba cut that chunk of dark hair out of my head.

I just hope it's not too late.

Love,
P

17

By the time I get to Barnaby's, Cendrillon is already there, dressed to the nines as usual—patent-leather burgundy Louboutins, long flowy yellow slacks, a deep violet silk button-down with a yellow bra underneath. She tosses her copper highlights away from her shoulders and slips out of her chair to greet me.

"Hi, Poppy. How are you?" She leans over to give me a hug. Cendrillon is thin, but her hold feels all-encompassing, like how I want my mother's embrace to feel. Where Cendrillon feels open, my mother felt cloistering, taking the breath out of me. I don't know what it is, but something in Cend expands the air in my chest.

"I've been better." I bite my lower lip. It's too early for tears. I didn't tell her much on the phone, just that I needed her. I was struck by how quickly she was able to be there for me.

Barnaby Café is a chain of restaurants spread throughout Houston. They started in Montrose. It's where you live if you're queer, artist, hipster, eccentric, or young. But, Montrose has changed—it's less queer now, more congested. Now there are stories—not always, but still too often—of yuppy bros who've moved into Montrose waiting at gay bars at 2 a.m. ready to pounce. Apparently it used to feel like the safest place to be a young queer, the only place you could really count on. Even Mary's (whose full name was It's Mary's ... Naturally), which catered to gay men, closed. It was the oldest gay bar in Houston, often employed go-go dancers, and regularly sponsored HIV/AIDS fundraising. Its exterior mural of its regulars lounging around a bar and playing pool was once something of a landmark for Montrose, they say. Now it, too, is just some hipster coffee shop for the straighties who don't even know what Montrose used to be once.

Even still, when I want to feel safe, Barnaby's is one of my go-tos.

"Hey, boo! How you doin'?"

Matt's got the dinner shift tonight. The right side of his blond hair is buzzed short, the other side is long, dyed bright pink. He gently drags his long fingernails against my shoulder, smiles.

"Oh, I'm okay, how you doin'? How's David?"

Cendrillon watches our interaction with affection.

"Oh, he's good. Takin' my life away, what else is new?" We laugh. It feels good to laugh, even if it's partly an act to hide the sadness I feel.

"I bet! Oh, this is my friend, Cendrillon. Cendrillon, this is Matt. He's my favorite. But don't tell anyone, I don't want them to get jelly." I nudge him with an elbow.

"Aw, girl. You're too sweet to me. Nice to meet you. Whatcha girls havin'?"

Cendrillon and I both order a coffee, and I order my favorite dessert for us to share, apple pie à la mode in a glass bowl. I order it to remind me of my mother's Southern ways, so that I can feel close to her, even when she makes me angry, because it makes her feel not so achingly far away.

One summer, I stayed with Mom half-time on my own. She'd been gone a lot around then—traveling to Florida and Italy and who knows where else. She would send us postcards, tell us in a line or two about all the adventures she was having. When she returned, she wanted to split custody with Baba again. Lola and Clark refused. They hadn't forgiven her for leaving. I felt bad for her. Staying with her, even part-time, was a challenge. She was out all the time, and Baba forbade me from staying at her apartment when she wasn't home.[23] When she went out at night, she made me promise to lie to Baba in the event that he called to check on me. My weekends were filled with anxiety the size of my missing mother because she almost never came home at night and never left a note and never called. I sat on the floor biting my nails into dust, hoping that each morning that she was gone when I awoke was like all the other mornings and nothing more serious had happened.

But, on the weekdays, since it was summer, I would wake early, well before her. I would make her coffee and pour in the cream just like she liked it, waiting until the coffee turned the shade of honey. I still made my coffee the same way. It was the only thing just ours, even when she often ruined the moment with her scatterbrained impatience from waking up late and rushing.

But perhaps it wasn't even sharing it with my mother I loved about it the most. I loved how the sun painted the wooden breakfast table and the cups of coffee canary-yellow and how the mornings felt so full of promise. Empty of disappointment, the day full and round and open. Anything could happen. The world so quiet and still. No Lola or Clark yelling, no Baba with his menacing threats. Each morning the world empty of the darkness that would soon, inevitably, fill the room, the house, the world. But not yet. Just my honey-tinged porcelain cup of coffee and the sunlight and the quiet that washed over me like a lavender bath.

23 If apartment catch fire, they all go down like domino.

Eating at Barnaby's used to be like this. I'd do it alone, with a book, happy as could be, checked up on by waiters I knew sitting at my favorite booth in the back corner. But then Lola found out about it, so now when I went there, the staff made jokes instead, like "how do I know you're not playing a prank on me and you really just walked out and walked right back in?" Just like that, I became unknown to them. I did what I always did where Lola was concerned. I withdrew myself from the competition. I let Lola have it. But when Cendrillon texted me back asking me where I wanted to go, I didn't think about Lola this time. I just thought about me.

We're halfway through the pie and on our second cup of coffee. I tell Cendrillon everything. I tell her about Lola disappearing, about the letters, about Peter and Paolo, about Mom leaving and Baba doing nothing, about his wife fleeing the country. I tell her that Clark hasn't made a peep. I tell her about my fears, that Paolo and Lola have run away together, that we've lost her for good. I tell her about my other fear, that Juniper will leave for school and I'll be stuck here. Forever. And then I tell her about Baba finding the letter, about what's led me here.

"Wow. Poppy. That's a lot to handle on your own. You're still so young, too. I'm just so glad you reached out to me." Cendrillon runs her nails through her hair.

"I'm so sorry to just unload on you like this, it's just—" My voice falters. I hide my face in my napkin.

"Hey, hey." Cendrillon gently grabs the napkin and pushes it down, so she can see my face. "Don't apologize. I'm just taking a minute to process all of this. I don't want to treat this lightly. This is just. It's just a lot for a young woman to deal with and I want to make sure I think about what I'm going to say. Okay?"

I take a beat. “Okay. Yeah. I totally get that.” I rub my hand over my eye, take another bite of pie.

“Poppy, what are you thinking? Like, what do you want to do? What’s your gut telling you?” She takes my hand. It doesn’t feel romantic. It feels like what a mother’s hand might feel like. Like love.

“I mean, I’ve been wanting to stay around in case Lola came back. What if she comes back and I’m not there? But, I’m not her parent. I can’t make Baba take this seriously. And you know, he has a point. She’s eighteen. What would we be able to do anyway? So. I don’t know. Part of me just wants to get out, when Juniper gets back. I just can’t believe Lola’s really gone.”

The tears gush forward. Cendrillon strokes my hand.

“I mean, I just, I guess I hadn’t really wanted to believe it. That she could really be gone forever. She’s been gone two months already, and we haven’t heard one peep from her. It just seems unthinkable that I wouldn’t know where my own twin was, if she’s sick, or happy, or trapped. My breath feels caught in my throat.”

Cendrillon inches her chair over to mine, and I nestle my face against her pristine silk blouse and weep until my cheek sticks against its damp surface. It feels good to get it out with someone who loves me.

After I’m empty of tears, I lift my head. Luckily Barnaby’s is dark, and Matt knows to let me be after so many years.

Cendrillon places a hand on my shoulder and looks into my eyes with gravity.

“Okay, look. A long time ago I had to do something similar, for very different reasons, when I was not that much older than you are now. I’ll miss you, of course. But, I think for your safety, for your well-being, you need to get out of here. You’re right. If your parents aren’t willing to search for her, you can’t really do much. At least you can leave Houston knowing you did all you could for her. It's my opinion Lola needs serious help. I don't even know if your family could afford the help she needs. But, you can't be responsible for her. You can only be responsible for you. And for your new life with Juniper. Like you said about Lola, you're eighteen, too. Your father can't stop you. And I think given his past abuse with all of you, this thing with Lola is only going to exacerbate his rage. I honestly don't think it's safe for you to stay there. When is Juniper coming home?"

"Tomorrow morning."

Cendrillon nods, all business. "Okay, then I think the minute she lands, you and Juniper should make a plan. Okay? I'm always here if you need me. I'm just a text or phone call away. Let me know if I can help in any way."

18

I don't really know how I'm going to get myself together before picking up Juniper from the airport. Back home, the blues turn into a tar that coats my body. I don't know how to get out of it. I have one letter left to write. And then I'm done. After talking to Cendrillon, I know it's what has to happen. To be done. Absolute detachment. I've spent enough time grieving her. I need to move on.

Last night when I got home from Barnaby's, Baba screamed at me like he did in the bad days, his voice crackling white: "This isn't hotel! You can't check in check out whenever you want. You need stay home with me. Study. You going to be like your sister too, just everyone always leaving me? You fucking assholes. I swear, no appreciation." But this time, I didn't do what I always did, standing in front of him silently weeping while he continued to scream and thrash around, hoping if I stayed still long enough, he would stop. I had no more tears for him. I just looked him in the face and then without saying a word, I stepped away from him, walked upstairs to my room, and quietly closed the door behind me.

Goddamn, I needed Juniper to come home. I just didn't feel safe when she wasn't within a drive's reach. Knowing Juniper was so far away made Baba's unpredictable mood swings and rage even more frightening, made me feel even more susceptible to his shifting violent eruptions. Where would I go if things escalated enough to need to leave before she got home? It was too scary to think about.

I don't want to go downstairs until it's time to leave for the airport but I'm tired of flipping through social media. I plug my headphones into my phone, and click on the YouTube link Juniper texted me the other day with the message:

> Pops. Watch every minute of this right this second. Well, it's a little long, so as soon as you can!

It's a film of Sufjan Stevens performing his 2015 album *Carrie & Lowell* in its entirety, an album he made to process his grief about his abandoning, mentally ill mother and his stepfather. Of the album, he said, "this is not my art project; this is my life."

I already played the entire hour-and-a-half video when I first woke up, missing Juniper and wanting to feel her with me. Not only that, but feeling embraced by the words of the album that feel so closely tethered to my own experience of grief, abandonment, loss, and love. After watching the film from front to end, I search for the music video for "Should Have Known Better," my favorite track on the album, letting myself be taken away by the images of the ocean and the bridges, taken away by the fantasy of being transported to a different life as I listen to Sufjan's lilting voice set against the delicate fingerpicking:

I should have wrote a letter
And grieve what I happen to grieve
My black shroud
I never trust my feelings
I waited for the remedy

And when I was three, maybe four
She left us at that video store
Be my rest, be my fantasy

I let the tears come, let myself feel the sadness of being lost, of being left, of failing Lola, of possibly never being able to move on from it. And then:

I'm light as a feather
I'm bright as the Oregon breeze
My black shroud
Frightened by my feelings
I only wanna be a relief

I want to hold on to it, the idea of lightness, to remind myself of relief as an answer, or a way of being.

And then there it was. Juniper. And Kai. And Cendrillon.

But. But.

JuniperJuniperJuniperJuniperJuniperJuniper.

And then, as suddenly as I thought it would crumble to dust, it is there, like a cleaning agent wiping away the tar. Hope. And that one-winged dove.[24]

24 "Drawn to the Blood," Sufjan Stevens.

19

I'll never forget this night. I'm still my thinky self,[25] but Juniper inflates me like I'm a bright red balloon. Airborne, letting the whim of the wind and the clouds take me wherever they want me to go. But, it isn't just Juniper's mind-blowingly wonderful homecoming I won't forget. I won't forget dancing and singing in the park at night. I danced to songs that spoke to my whole life, to the darkness and sadness of the concrete-white suburbs, to the love I share with Juniper, to the singing, the singing, the singing, I would always sing, that was for sure, and with each note that rang out of my mouth, I rewrote each song that had been written for another purpose and another time into the story so I could be of the world and in the world and above the world and beneath the world. I freed her and I healed myself from the notes I sang. It didn't matter I wasn't the most perfect singer. All that mattered is that when I sang, the world felt better. A world I could believe in, a world that gave me song, while Juniper stood behind me and wrapped her arms around my waist.

25 "Think, think, think!" Winnie-the-Pooh's musing which turned into his signature move.

20

My phone has buzzed incessantly for the last three hours. I'm trying to ignore it, to be with Juniper and the feeling of being part of something beyond that house and its multitudes. But as usual, Baba always gets in the way. Juniper's different. She's been to the other side of the world, to a place where queer people don't have to hide, a place where even your parents can't touch you. I can already see a lightness in Juniper even after just a week away. She's giddy, not just about being around so many people like her, but also about being around the lush landscape and the bowing trees in a summer wind far away from everything.

But, it's hard to focus. Baba has called, then texted, then called, then texted, every fifteen minutes for over two hours. I'd left him a note when I went to pick up Juniper, with an excuse I'd hoped would work, but as it became well after midnight, he was starting to figure it out, that I was slipping through his fingers, too.

As we held each other while sitting on Kai's bedroom floor watching our favorite, *Saving Face*, after Kai's parents had gone to bed, I could feel the heat of Juniper's protective anger building. Her shoulders rising, her face tightening. Sometimes Kai would look down on us from where he sat on his bed and ask if everything was okay. But we all knew it wasn't.

When I was fifteen, before I met Juniper, I went to homecoming stag with my straight white friend Lisa. On our way home her phone died and I'd nodded off. While I slept, she circled around the same three streets of the suburb where we lived with Baba. When she finally decided to wake me to tell me she was lost, it was too late. We were five minutes from my house when a cop pulled us over for curfew. The cop tried to take me to the station since I didn't have a license,[26] but I cried and flailed and screamed knowing the hell that already faced me and how much worse it would be if Baba had to pick me up at the police station. The officer let me go with a ticket instead. Of course Lisa, blonde and freckled, was given only a warning.

When I finally got home, my hands and legs shook from what I knew awaited me. This, of course, wouldn't have happened at all if Lola had let me go home with her like originally planned. But Lola wouldn't stand for a third wheel, especially not one who shared her face. I tried to open the door quietly. Not that it mattered. All of the lights downstairs were on and a blanket was draped over the sofa. Baba had worn spirals into the carpet from his pacing. Just like the Uzumaki curse.

At first, he didn't say a word. He just stared at me. And then "I about to call the police" and "you sleep outside" and "tǎo yàn a" and "you go see if your mother have pity on you and take you in I doubt she will" and paper cuts slashed across each cheek where he chucked the curfew ticket at my face. If his wife hadn't been there, Baba would have had me sleep outside in the windswept dark. Instead, Baba's wife intervened: "That's too much. Poppy, you go wash your face and go to sleep. You're safe now, you're home. That's all that matters. Tài duō le."

The night of the curfew ticket I washed my face after he had exhausted himself and gone to bed. I put Neosporin on the little

26 I'd only barely been able to convince my father that I needed one since a license meant power and power was something my father wanted all to himself.

red lines the ticket left on my cheeks and went to bed. I sobbed all night at the idea it could be that easy to become homeless, that easy for him to throw his own child out in the street. I sobbed because I wished Mom had the kind of life or time to keep me safe from him. I was stuck with Baba, never knowing when he would blow up next.

He apologized the night we had to go to court to pay the ticket, but I knew. I knew his wife made that apology happen. I knew he was apologizing to keep her in his life, to keep his wife from walking out on him for being so cruel to his daughter. He was not apologizing because he cared. If only I'd thought about how the fear inside that house might have been greater than any I could find on the streets.

But, this isn't a school dance. I'm not fifteen anymore. He can't do anything to keep me here. Just like he couldn't do anything to make Lola stay.

Juniper stops the film, shifts herself to rest her back against the wall. She runs a hand through her hair, checks the silver watch on her left wrist. Her other hand rests on my shoulder. It is soft, but thrums with questions. She looks at me, then at Kai.

"What should we do? I guess we have to deal with it. Should I take you home?"

Kai doesn't say anything, but waits to see what I will do.

I don't want the night to end and I don't want to leave Juniper. Not when she's finally back. I'm afraid of what I'll find on the other side of the door if I go home. The fear is a big blank hole I can fill with the unimaginable, and somehow, all the scenarios are possible. I haven't even told her my plans. We hadn't even gotten that far before Baba started texting.

Juniper watches me. She can see my mind swirl.

"I haven't even gotten to tell you. I was just trying to bask in the light of our reunion before getting into all that crap."

"Tell me what? Did something happen? Is everything okay? Pops?"

"Oh, Juniper. I don't know where to start."

Juniper looks up at Kai to see if he knows. He shakes his head and shrugs without saying a word.

But I do. I tell her what it's been like while she's been gone. I tell her about the letters, how much I miss Lola, how much I ache for where she might be. I tell her about the last time Paolo came after Lola, how I thought we'd dodged a bullet. And then she was gone. I tell her about my confrontation with Baba. That he's never going to do anything. Of course he won't. I tell her how angry I am that Mom took off. I tell her about meeting Cendrillon, how she thinks we should get the hell out of here.

It takes me a while to get through it all. Sometimes my tears are quiet, just lonely drops rolling down my doubled cheeks. And sometimes my tears are loud and full of so many whimpers that Juniper can't understand the words trying to break through. I have to stop, collect myself, and begin again. But, I get through it, even as the whole time that I'm telling her what I know we must do, Baba continues to call, text, call, text. I could silence my phone. But it feels important to know what lies in wait as a reminder of what staying would be like.

Juniper doesn't say anything for a minute or two. Neither do I. We just sit in it, holding one another.

Finally, Juniper clears her throat. When she does that, I know she means business. I know a decision is ahead. It coats me with relief, and the feeling of not being alone.

"You know, I don't want to be here any more than you do. My parents are fucked, too. You know that. Especially my mom. I'm going to Smith, and you probably can, too. I have money saved.

Why don't we just leave now?"

"But. What if our parents call the cops?"

"They won't. This is about your dad not being in control. He's just a bully. But why don't you send him a letter. Or you could even tape it to the front door tomorrow before we head out. Say the things he never lets you say. I'll do that, too, actually. I was gonna wait to come out until I got to college, but fuck it. Let's do it."

All I know is I don't want to think about it anymore.

Juniper holds my chin up so my eyes can't shift around. I sigh.

"Yeah. This could work. Okay. We're eighteen. What can they do? If anything, this whole Lola thing just proves they won't do anything. I heard Baba say on the phone he has a meeting with the production team tomorrow morning, so we'll stop by then and get the essentials. Let's just start driving."

21

I wake in a land of stories and freedom. In this new land, time no longer means what it used to, and a quiet falls around me. I wake in the kind of happiness your brain collages into dreams, skin glowing from a glass of shining joy you drink up just before you realize it's your mind imagining the best of what the world might offer you, just before you realize it's a dream, a dream, only a dream.

But.

But.

It's not a dream. I'm here, in a sleeping bag on the floor of Kai's room, with the girl I love, who chooses to share sleep and song and sweetness with me. Not even Lola can take her away. And this girl I love picks me against all odds, and even Baba's rage isn't too much for her to bear. Even possibly being disowned by her mother for loving me isn't too much to bear. In fact, with the weight of queer community and the landscape of New England behind her, Juniper almost welcomes the danger Baba promises. It's as though I have new skin, free of its wounding past.

I open my eyes and look around me. Juniper's face a lullaby, her eyes twitch slowly awake. It amazes me how different a space can feel. The whole room, even on the slippery material of the sleeping bag, the hardness of Kai's carpeted floor, still tingles with the magic I associate with our life together. My head might as well be nestled on a baby lamb. I stretch my legs as far as they extend, stretching and hyperextending my arms in the opposite direction, moaning softly. Juniper turns towards me and readjusts, her head now in between my thigh and waist, her silky hand fingering the waistband of my boy shorts. She kisses me just below my belly button as she draws circles on the curve of my lower back. I shiver. What world could be better than this one?

As my sigh turns, Juniper squints up at me, her eyes still resisting the day.

"Poptart?"

"Hi Junebug!"

I squeal a little too loud for how early it is, for how unready Juniper is to face the morning. Oops. I don't want to wake up Kai. Not yet.

"Say it again. I want to remember this morning forever. My Poppy out of that dungeon and in my arms. And us, so soon, forever away from the parents who tried to rip us apart."

I close my eyes and grin. And then I do as she asks. Again and again and again. Until Kai wakes up anyway, and starts teasing us until my face turns apple red.

The three of us spend the morning in our pajama bottoms and tanks, slowly enjoying the coffee Juniper made sitting at the bar in the kitchen. While Kai takes a shower, Juniper tells me all about Northampton, the campus, and the wild coincidence of finding the *Uzumaki* book at the one bookstore she popped into, but also about the meetings and the profs and the department. I just let it wash over me, all her excitement and chatter of the days we'd been apart. I don't disrupt the moment with worries about the future for once, and Juniper takes the unusual airtime to fill it with words and happiness and noise free of agitation. All that matters right now is I'm here, away from Baba and from the letters and his house and the sadness that has always been synonymous with my life. I try to imagine this new life, one where I live with my sweetheart and wake up every morning when we're ready to accompany the sun, and I make breakfast while Juniper makes the bed, and we chat and read and sometimes drift into each other's thoughts and sometimes share those thoughts with one another until we have to start the day and one takes a shower while the other keeps her company, only a shower curtain or a glass door separating us. And the days move into the nights, and the weeks move into the months, and soon a life is made like this, sprouting from moments like last night, when we finally said no to the barriers keeping us apart.

I move in and out of Juniper's monologue, enjoying all the stories and her excitement over the trip's success and then wafting in and out as I daydream about a life I assumed I would never get the chance to lead and then coming back to the present moment I am lucky enough to have and waft out again.

"So, Popcorn ... um..."

Juniper nervously scratches her head as discomfort sketches across her face, once we've finished our coffee and newspaper.

"Yeah, what is it?"

"I have a few things to take care of."

"What things?" My eyebrows furrow to a V.

Juniper giggles, tousling my hair. "Oh, don't you even worry about it! Besides, I know you still need to bring the letter over to Baba and get your things, right? It's a lot, I know. More for you than for me. But we'll make a time to meet up soon? Just get ready for our big adventure! Maybe if you have time, you can even make us a playlist!"

"Yeah I know. I'm not looking forward to it. I just hope he's not there." I scan her eyes to make sure I can file the worries away.

"Me, too. So much. In the meantime, I'm here when you need me, and I'll turn the volume WAY UP on my phone so I make sure to hear. Please call me if there's an emergency. I'll text you in a couple hours, okay?"

We kiss. Juniper caresses my face with her hand.

"Everything will be okay. Okay?" She peers into my eyes, just like I'd done a moment before. I'd never really had anyone look me in the eye like that before, concern untied to guilt or selfishness. I wasn't the victim being rescued by a hero. We were both survivors. Both heroes.

After I watch Juniper pull out of Kai's driveway, I find Kai in his room, and ask if I can take a bath before I take off to Baba's house. "Take your time," he tells me after giving me a long hug. I take a long bath with the eucalyptus spearmint oil on the rim of Kai's bathtub, the same kind I sent with Juniper on her trip to Smith to help keep her calm for her campus tour, and play all the songs on my phone that remind me of us. I think about the metaphors of my life. I think about the narcissistic scientist whose mother finds him a bride who she also calls his cousin,[27] a beautiful child with golden ringlets born into a family too poor to care for her properly, a child who was eventually struck with scarlet fever and who then healed herself by transferring her infection to Frankenstein's mother. And I think about this child who never recovered from his mother's death and who needed very much to believe that death could be reversed, and so he made this body by animating the body parts of the dead, but really it was his mother he wanted back, merely her death he

27 "I have a pretty present for my Victor—tomorrow he shall have it."

wanted to reanimate back to life.[28] I think about the creature this scientist made that wandered into the woods and came upon his own hideous image, who learned how to speak and how to read and how to educate himself, and who, just so he could be loved by someone, loved first a family he scavenged for, out of love and out of hope of recognition. I think about the woman who made the story of the sad scientist and his dead mother and his sad monster but also about the mother of the woman who made this story who had also died when her daughter was four days old, who she would never know. I think about Cendrillon who asked me with her typical unassuming insight if there was any of this saddened, narcissistic scientist in my own obsessing over this book again and again and again, and I'd said, "No, of course not, I'm Mary Shelley," and Cendrillon had, gently, as always, pushed me to seek the real answer to that question: "Mary Shelley's too easy. It's the easiest identification, the most flattering." And I said, "Well, I'm also the abandoned child, I'm the monster." And Cendrillon pushed me further. "Yes, but that's also obvious. Go deeper. It's not possible, I don't think, for you to fixate on a novel like *Frankenstein* and not, at least somehow, have a subconscious identification with Frankenstein. I mean, I think we all have it in us. But you. You, too, Poppy, are Frankenstein." I think about how I fought against it but that line—"The beauty of the dream vanished, and breathless horror and disgust filled my heart"—something in that line. It was Lola. Lola was my monster—she wasn't a monster I had made, but a creature I'd spent my entire life trying to remake into something else, something better, something untouched by monsters.

28 "I had worked hard for nearly two years, for the sole purpose of infusing life into an inanimate body. For this I had deprived myself of rest and health. I had desired it with an ardour that far exceeded moderation; but now that I had finished, the beauty of the dream had vanished, and breathless horror and disgust filled my heart."

I'd written letter after letter. I'd tried to save Lola from the disaster I could see befall her, but in the end I just couldn't. And in Lola's destruction, I saw something of my own demise. I saw myself: her face, her body, but with different markers, different movements, different behavior. I didn't have to wonder what it would be like to open the door with the lion behind it. Lola was the lion. Lola was the cautionary tale. And I carried an immense guilt in having that privilege, in seeing what my body would make of disaster, what it would turn into, but without having turned. I just couldn't do it anymore.

And then, out of nowhere, I think of *Pinocchio*. When I was sixteen, I'd driven down to Brazos, the indie bookstore in town, and bought this book of paintings accompanied by the original story that inspired the paintings, the one written by the Italian children's writer, *Storia di un burattino* (The story of a marionette), published in the first Italian newspaper for children. And for a time, I had been as obsessed with this children's story, written just seventy years after the story of the mad scientist, as I had with *Frankenstein*, and suddenly, here in the bathtub which has run cold with all of my spiraling thoughts, I think of the carpenter who first came across the piece of wood that became the puppet named Pinocchio,[29] and the carpenter, hearing the piece of wood cry out when he tried to turn it into furniture, exclaiming: "Is it possible that this piece of wood can have learned to cry and to lament like a child?" I think about Baba, who is also a carpenter, and who loved his pieces of wood as though they were the children he'd always wanted to have instead of me and Lola and Clark. I think about how the two of us, his twin girls, had also become puppets in his hand, or planks of wood. If a piece of wood can learn to cry and lament like a child, perhaps a child can be

29 "How it came to pass that Master Cherry the carpenter found a piece of wood that laughed and cried like a child."

taught to become as frozen and subservient as a piece of wood.

Baba's car is in the driveway. Too late to turn back now.

I decide to come into the house through the front this time, hoping that maybe he is working and he won't hear me.

But, just like the night when I got the curfew ticket, Baba is walking back and forth from the living room to the study. I recognize the lines he wears into the carpet, just like last time. This isn't going to be pretty.

I can see dark circles under Baba's eyes, his hair disheveled, as though he's only just woken up. He has an air of defeat that disarms me. I'm not used to it. The look of him makes me nervous, but it's a different kind of nervous than what I usually feel around him. It's a vulnerability I don't recognize.

"Hi, guāi-guāi. Come sit down. We talk," Baba says, as he sits in the armchair across from the TV, and gestures to the nearby sofa. I knew it was possible I would run into Baba when I went in to leave the letter and grab a few of my things that I couldn't live without, but this is not the version of him I expected to find.

"Okay," I say, and I can hear my voice shake as I make my way to sit on the sofa, my legs trembling.

"Listen. I know I haven't been best father. I should have talked to you about things. I should have pay more attention to you and Lola around my friends. Your stepmother when I went to visit, we talked a lot about things. She told me long time ago about Peter that she see something happening, but I just didn't want to believe it. I thought, you girls American, you know, affectionate. And then after, I guess I thought it was over. I don't see you when you with your mother, I don't know what she does. I know she have friends like to party. But I know now. I should have pay more attention."

Baba is looking me in the face, something he rarely does. But I can't look back. It's too much. So my eyes flitter to him a second here or there, but stay focused on the goosebumps on my legs, the hairs standing straight up. I've wanted to hear some version of what he's saying for so long. Now that it's here, I don't know what to do with it.

He clears his throat briefly.

"I know this my fault. Okay. That's what Baba want to say. What do you want to say? Say whatever you want to say to me. Sometime we just need to talk," Baba says, forcing a smile that looks out of sync on him. I appreciate that he's trying.

"Well. I mean. I really appreciate what you said, so much," I start, my eyes tearing. "I just. I know Năinai was hard on you. I know you can't help what you do. But it's so hard to be so scared all the time. And I wish you would fight harder to find her. I can't do it by myself. I need you, Baba," I say to him, my voice clear in the beginning, but ending in a whisper. I squeeze my eyes shut tight.

"It's okay," he says to me, and wraps his arms around me in a hug, one of the few he's ever given me. I let it happen, without fighting it.

22

I wake to ringing. I'm lying awkwardly on the edge of the bed, the skin covering my cheekbones crusted over with tears. My phone beeps three times in rapid succession. Juniper. An hour before I'd fallen asleep, Juniper had texted to check in on me.

I could tell it was hard for Juniper to see me filled with doubt about Baba suddenly, especially after everything he'd done. She never tried to change my mind, though; she wasn't like me. Juniper never felt she had the power to change someone, especially when it involved something as big and unwieldy and complicated as a father like Baba was. Juniper had a cruel mother, too, so she knew how large the pain loomed, how impossible it was to solve.

When I called Juniper, I told her what had happened. I didn't know how to leave him right when he had finally given me a sliver of what I wanted, him taking responsibility for some of the tragedies of Lola's disappearance and everything else that might have caused her to leave us. Juniper didn't really know what to do with all that, so I could feel her slowly falling away from me, turning inward. I worried I'd ruined everything, that I'd ruined our future. But I felt caught between the past and the future, the Baba I wanted and the Juniper I needed.

"So what are you saying exactly?" Juniper asked after I told her what Baba had said, her voice flat and cold.

"I don't know. I just feel like I owe it to Baba, and to Lola, to see this through, I guess. After wanting so much for Baba and Mom to make all this right, doesn't it seem wrong to just leave? Aren't I just like Lola if I do that now, now that we're finally making progress? I need you, Juniper. You have to know that."

Juniper fell silent on the other end of the phone. I wondered if I was making the biggest mistake of my life.

"Look, Pops. You do what you have to do. Personally, I think he knows he's on the verge of losing you, and he's scrambling. I can't imagine how you're feeling, though, and I'm sure that felt so good to hear. I'm just worried about you. But, I don't know. I worked my whole life around in order for us to leave, mostly to keep you safe. So I'm at a loss of what to do now."

I wanted them both. I wanted Baba to love me, to fight to find Lola, to apologize for everything he did. But I wanted Juniper by my side, too. Maybe I didn't deserve to have it all.

I wanted to suggest we take a walk together and hash this out, but before I could say anything, Juniper interrupted me.

"Hey, look, I'm gonna get off the phone. I think I just need a minute to myself. Okay?"

"Okay," I said, because I didn't know what else there was to say. She hung up before I got a chance to think of something else to say to keep her on the line. Anything.

I stared blankly at the phone in my hand for the longest time. My bones ached with a cold burn.

When we weren't okay, when we weren't Poppy and Juniper taking on the world one cascading giggle at a time, I wasn't okay. I could deal with anything in the world, as long as I could prepare for it. As long as Juniper was there to help me through it.

I sit up. I walk to the bathroom, throw cold water on my face. After we'd been together for a week, I looked up Juniper's sun sign on an astrology website. I don't remember all of it, but there was always this one part that stuck with me, because it was essential Juniper: "Their empathy and compassion means they sense where others are coming from, and so can relate on a certain level. Their awareness of others gives them the ability to deal with any situation, and they do well in any area which involves understanding others."[30] Juniper always knew. But now I didn't know how to get back to what we were without losing everything else in the process.

I should have known better.

I don't know what it was I was hoping for when Baba said a version of the words I'd waited to hear for so long.

Did I think it was that easy to mend a lifetime?

Did I think that was all it took?

Oh, how I wanted it to be that easy. But that's not my story—not mine, or Lola's.

It's been a week since my world turned colorless, since Juniper and I fell away from each other. I just wish I knew how to get her back.

Each day turned into the next without warning. The letters were almost done. Juniper and I were at a standstill. I'd seen Cendrillon once since that day, and although she listened with understanding, I could see in her eyes that she thought I was making a mistake. She was too kind to say it to my face, but I saw her eyebrow

30 www.starslikeyou.com

carve out a question mark. I had the same question. I was just at a loss as to how to answer.

I was waiting. Waiting for Baba to come to me with a plan for how to find Lola. Waiting for the moment of the apology to mean something, to shift us into a new place we'd never been before.

But the shift never happened. We went through each day as we always did—mostly silent, eating dinners together, Baba asking me how much I'd studied that day. He seemed content, as though now everything could go back to the way it always was. But how could we go back when Lola was still gone? What was taking him so long to realize that as long as she was gone, things would never be what they were? What was he waiting for?

And then, one day, I just couldn't wait anymore.

I waited until Baba brought after-dinner fruit to the table, after eating beef noodle soup, one of my favorites of his home-cooked meals, a close second to jiǎozi. I didn't start talking until he was busy eating a juicy chunk of papaya and couldn't interrupt me.

"Baba?" I started, trying to get up the nerve.

"Hmm?" he said through chewing.

"So what are we gonna do to find Lola? You have ideas?" I decided to assume our goal was the same, united by a common bond of finding our lost one.

Baba swallowed, scratched his head. "Oh, uh. I just..." His voice drifted off. I waited for him to continue.

"You are gonna look for her, right?" I could hear my voice rise in pitch and volume, my chest sticky and hot.

"Well, uh, I just think if she want to come home, she come home, right? I mean, she an adult now. I don't think anything I can really do." He brought his attention back to the fruit, a distraction that enraged me further.

"You're not going to do anything?!" I kicked my chair back. It clattered backwards on the bamboo floor, more dramatic than I intended.

"Everything you said," I began, my voice caught in my throat, "it didn't mean anything, did it?"

Without waiting for an answer, I ran upstairs to my room, grabbed my laptop, the overnight bag I'd packed just in case I needed to run out in an emergency. Baba screamed at me to face him, but there was nothing left to face. I got in my car and started driving without aim or destination. Sometimes, it's enough just to know what you're running from.

But, what was it I was staying for, anyway? It's not as though I hadn't known, in a way no other child of the family had known, who Baba was and who Mom was and who Lola was. But it didn't matter. I would always hope tomorrow would bring the promise of a better life. It reminded me of this movie about a privileged white lesbian couple with two children from the same sperm donor. Their world falls apart when the daughter makes contact with him after her eighteenth birthday. He does terrible things, it's all a mess, and at the end of it the daughter says to the sperm donor who suddenly wants so badly to be a father: "I just wish that you could have been [and he says "what?" when she doesn't finish her sentence] ... better."[31] I'd always want Baba to be better. I'd want him to deal with his rage. I'd want him to refuse the impulse that stemmed from his hand. I'd want him to want us to be happy, no matter how it made him look, no matter what he thought of it. I'd want him to be able to bond with us. I'd want him to care about giving us a world of peace and safety and

31 *The Kids Are All Right.*

freedom over anything else. Most of all, I'd want him to want to protect us.

But.

But.

He would never be any of these things. Somewhere I knew that. But now, I had a new hope to worry about keeping alive, the hope I had for Juniper and me to live a different life. I hoped the hope wasn't like the one about the two of us, me and Lola, and that ours wouldn't also end up stillborn.

But, here's the thing. The world is telling me it is time to let go, to grieve everything: Baba, Mom, especially Lola, to grieve what they will never be. Or to grieve what I can never be for them. That was always the problem with Frankenstein. He never allowed himself to grieve his mother, and he never confronted the ugliness of himself he saw in the thing he created. And so Frankenstein and his monster, they both lived in unrest until Frankenstein died on a boat in the bitter cold, all of his loved ones snuffed out by the very thing he created to give the world life. You can't stop the world from charting its own course, all you can do is rechart your own path by letting go of the course you wanted so desperately but you know is not to be.

I drive into town to get a bite to eat at Barnaby's. Just after I manage to get out of the suburbs in one piece, I pull over on a side street before the feeder to the freeway and send Juniper a text:

> I don't know if you're here or there, but I'm sorry. You were right, as always. He's never gonna be what I want. I miss you and I love you. I'll be at Barnaby's if you want to talk. I hope you do.

I do my thing. I breathe in, I stretch my shoulders and round them back, I roll my head around my neck, I try to cast all the disappointments away from me. I look down at my phone but the screen remains blank. I hope Juniper still wants me along for our fairytale.

Just as I'm wrapping up dinner, Kai texts me.

> Hey boo, how are you holding up? Juniper told me you finally got the hell outta dodge! I think Juniper's still thinking through things, but I'm sure she'll come around! Can I come see you?

Although I'm disappointed it's not Juniper checking in, I'm thrilled to hear from a friend. Please, would you??? I could use one of your epic hugs.❤

I ask for another cup of coffee while I wait for Kai to arrive—he says he's in town, so it shouldn't take too long.

I jaunt to the bathroom, fling some water on my face, apply my bright pink Fenty, smooth down my dress (just in case Juniper reaches out, I want to be prepared). Before I get back to the booth, Kai's texted again, telling me to meet him outside around the corner .

What I find there takes my breath. It's not Kai.

Instead, a little Corgi pup sits alone on the grass with a little Bluetooth speaker sitting next to her. A small handwritten sign hangs around her neck.

"WHAT THE!!!!!!!!!" I scream to no one but the puppy. I scoop her up and scratch her chin and cluck at her. "You're so adorable!" I squeal, overwhelmed with excitement at what this possibly means.

The sign reads: *Play me. Please press* PAUSE *after you play the first song.* I follow the instructions. The song is "Power of Two," by the Indigo Girls. It's the song I told Juniper I always wanted to have in my own airport love scene one day, when I never thought I'd find a Joey or Felicity or Angela or Blair. I don't know what to do with the moment I imagine might follow this one, my mouth agape, my eyes watering.

The ball of fur jumps out of my arms and runs to someone standing behind me. I swivel around and it's Juniper. Juniper Juniper Juniper Juniper. Sitting with her legs folded under one another on the grass, as though nothing has happened.

"Junebug...?" My voice barely creaks out a whisper.

"I've got a question for you," she grins.

"June! Are you sure? I'm so, so sorry about everything."

"Please, it's okay. I mean it," she says, holding my two hands together in hers. "But, enough of that. I'm just glad you're here, and you're done with that now. Will you run away with me? Please? I need a Poppy Uzumaki like an Emily needed a Maya."

I start to say yes, even through the tears, but Juniper beats me to it.

"If your answer is yes, I'm wondering if you'd do one more thing. Please hit PLAY. If you can answer yes, then you'll make me the happiest Juniper Kim in the world."

I do as Juniper requests. It's one of my songs this time, one I'd sung to her at night when she was too antsy to fall asleep during our stealthy sleepovers, and the singing had lightly caressed Juniper's skin and hair, and every time I thought Juniper had grown tired of it, she'd asked me to sing it again, and again, and again. Even though it was kind of an expected love song to sing, she still loved it anyway.

Troye Sivan croons "Youth" through the tiny speaker. It's Montrose, so sometimes queer couples walk by and stop, smiling at our love in one of the only places in the world we don't feel we have to hide it. Juniper wants me to stay. And she wants me to run away with her. Maybe forever.

August 20, 2019

Dear Baba,

I have nothing more to say that hasn't already been said. But I didn't want you to think I'm running away, like Lola did. So, I wanted to give you a heads-up.

I'm queer. And I'm running away with my girlfriend to college in Massachusetts.

I wish you would have fought harder for Lola. I wish you would have told Peter what he did was wrong. Even if we lost face.

Remember that time we had that breakfast at Classic Kitchen on Bellaire, with the big fried sticks we dipped in the huge warm bowl of soy milk? It took me forever to find out what it's called, but I've been reading this book about a girl like me, half-Chinese and half-white, who wrote about it, too. I found out it's called youtiao and it's a popular Taiwanese breakfast. Lola had spent the night with a friend. Not sure where Clark was, but it was just you and me, breaking bread together, softening it in the warm milk where sometimes your piece of bread and mine would touch. We didn't speak. I felt such tenderness towards you that day, from you. You asked me questions from time to time like you do - "how's the school? Study?" Sometimes you would take my bread, dip it for me. It felt like love. And I wanted everything to feel as simple as it did that day. But, I know better now. It's so much more complicated than that.

I've learned something this summer, probably the hardest thing I've ever had to learn. That I can't make you or Mom try harder. That I can't really do it on my own. And I can't make Lola be anything other than what she is. But every day I hope she's okay. I hope you will be, too.

Love,
Poppy

August 22, 2019

Dear Twin,

So here we are. Letter eighteen. I didn't actually think I'd make it this far.

I love you and I miss you.

I'm getting out of Baba's house. It's time. I tried so hard to get you back. But it's kinda hard to do it on my own. At some point, maybe I just need to accept your choices, and hope to god you aren't with Paolo.

I'm here for you. Whenever you need me. I'm sure I won't be hard for you to find.

And I hope wherever you are, you're not someone's trophy or victim. You deserve so much more than that. We both do.

When I look in the mirror and see that little freckle above my lip, I'll think of the one you have, the one on the other side that matches up to mine when we look one another in the face. When I think of that mole on the side of my head that you somehow managed not to get, too, I'll still think of you.

Love,
yr twin

Epilogue

I wake up to the sound of feet pattering around the house. Not just any feet. Indigo's and Juniper's feet as Indigo follows Juniper around the house while she gets ready. I stretch in our bed layered with the linens of fall (it's the second week of September, which means every inch of the house must signal *yes, yes, please, Halloween, won't you come?*).

We live in a house near campus in Northampton. We've been here a month already. I took out student loans (now that Baba is no longer in the picture, it didn't much matter he always threatened to disown any of his children who took money from the government) and declared a major in creative writing. Every day at 12:30, we share a picnic together on the large lawn on campus. Juniper's parents never responded to her coming-out letter. Juniper is still going through it. And Baba hasn't uttered a peep. Neither has Lola. We are working through our family shit together. As always. As ever.

Juniper's an architecture major, and she works way into the night most days on projects for class. It's a full and uncontainable life, and it's hard sometimes to see Juniper so little, especially during the week. But it gives me time to write the novel about the letters.

After I'd gotten the barest essentials from my room back

home, I'd sent that one last letter to Lola, along with a playlist[32] to demonstrate what being her twin had meant to me. And I'd left the letter on Baba's front door, too. Then Juniper and I got into her Honda and drove to our new home.

Lola was still my twin. I still felt unmoored without a resolution.

Juniper runs all over the house, trying to get ready for her first exam. It is 6:45.

"June-cake, calm down! Your exam isn't for four hours still!" I scream out to wherever in the house Juniper is off to next.

"You know how I get, Lollipop. I gotta get the highest grade of the whole class. Model Minority probs!" Juniper screams from downstairs.

"Very funny. You know you'll ace it with your eyes closed!"

Suddenly, Juniper's next to her side of the bed wearing her leather messenger bag, one of my pink dress shirts with a blue-and-white polka-dotted silk tie, black slacks, and dress shoes.

"Good morning, roomie!"

Juniper kisses me in a flash, her eyes boomeranging off the walls.

"Babe, relax! You're gonna do great!" I scratch the top of her head.

"Don't! I just put gel in it! Well, we'll see. But I gotta jet. I won't feel comfortable until I'm in the library crackin' the

32 1. "Part of Your World," *The Little Mermaid* soundtrack
2. "Emily," Joanna Newsom
3. "I'm Yours," Jason Mraz (a song Lola and I loved equally, and always reminded me of Lola, the good parts)
4. "Brave," Sara Bareilles
5. "Don't Let It Bring You Down," Annie Lennox
6. "Love Song," Sara Bareilles (one of Lola's favorite songs)
7. "Power of Two," Indigo Girls
8. "Sticky Teenage Twin," Snow Patrol
9. "I Wish I Had an Evil Twin," The Magnetic Fields
10. "Twin," Muse

books." She carefully primps her hair back into place.

"Okie dokie. Good luck! See you after on the lawn?" Even though it's our daily routine, I still have to make sure. It still stuns me Juniper is always where she promises to be.

"You know it, cute little poppy-seed cake always checking on things she doesn't need to. Good luck with the writing Poppy-do! When we get home today, let's hook you up with a website!"

And then, just like that, she scurries off.

After steamed jiǎozi that night, we scoot up to my laptop.

"Okay, cutie pie, let's get this shit DONE. I suggest poppyuzumaki.com and letterstoada.com. I'm gonna run downstairs and check the mail. Don't worry! I'll be back in a flash to help."

Juniper springs out of her chair and hops downstairs to the front door.

I type in www.poppyuzumaki.com. Hit SEARCH.

! Sorry, poppyuzumaki.com is not available. Still want it? Learn more.

I click MORE.

Registered by Lola Uzumaki on September 5th, 2019.

I try two other searches, including the working title for the book on Lola. Same.

My body leaves the chair. I don't notice Juniper standing behind me until I hear her gasp.

I turn towards Juniper. She holds an envelope in her hands.

"Poprocks? It's from your dad." She peers into my face.

I tear open the envelope. It's not from him, though. It's from Lola.

But before I can read it, Juniper eases it out of my hands, placing it face down on the desk. She falls to her knees and turns me towards her, cradling my face in her hands.

"Poppy? Before you read this, I want you to remember something. You have a new family now. You aren't alone anymore. And we have love, which makes us stronger than she can possibly imagine.[33] In other words, just say the word, and she's going down."[34]

33 *Punch-Drunk Love.*
34 Closing credits roll as "Pompeii," by Bastille, plays in the background.

Acknowledgments

This book has, like me, shifted and morphed and moved through so many births and so many bodies before finally landing on this one. I wrote this for those young and not-so-young bodies who feel invisible or lost, who come to define themselves by saving others and may forget themselves in the process, who find themselves living out someone else's story rather than their own. But, most of all, I wrote this for those who are twinned, who long to find their one amidst their two, for whom their journey is more than just a trope of look-alikes popping up in the background.

To my extraordinary editors and publishers, Ashley Fortier and Oliver Fugler, who not only took this baby from its toils and troubles and brought it to life, but who invested in it with love, thoughtfulness, heart, and understanding.

To Roxane Gay, CB Lee, Corey Whaley, Kiese Laymon, Emily Danforth, Alaina Leary, Nina Lacour, and my Binders community, who, in one way or another, gave this book the nurturing it needed at the beginning, pushed me forward when it seemed this book would not see the light of day, gave me the tough-love advice I needed to make sure I gave this book the environment in which it would most thrive.

To TC Tolbert, my brother and dearest family, a friend and a mentor, who was the first to embrace this book and publish the beginnings of Poppy's story with *The Feminist Wire*. So much love.

To Keet Geniza, who lovingly brought Poppy and Lola and Juniper to life in so many different incarnations, imbued with a sweetness and an understanding I could have never predicted or imagined.

To my queer Asian circle of love and trust and snacks, who I could not have gotten through this whirlwind bringing this book to the world without: Muriel Leung, Kay Ulanday Barrett, and Angela Peñaredondo.

To Mat Johnson, Kiese Laymon, Corey Whaley, Steven Chbosky, Marguerite Duras, Nina Lacour, Theresa Hak Kyung Cha, Anne Carson, Mary Shelley, for how you teach me to strive for your level of truth and abundance.

To Alexander Chee, who made me feel less alone, and gave me the courage to tell it true.

To Michelle Lamb, Joe Osmundson, and Pallavi Govindnathan, who gave me a sofa and a roof and so much more, when New York and Vermont were the two places the book needed to become complete.

To Sufjan Stevens, for the river to write alongside.

To Judy Blume, for teaching me that books could keep afloat adrift ones like me.

To Gizmo, for showing me one can find healing, home, family, magic, even twinning in the most unexpected places. I don't think I could have reached the finish line without you. Thank you for seeing me, and reminding me we can be our own life rafts.

To J, without whom this book could not exist.

To my twin, who, in pain and knowing, is part of the body I live in, despite the distance we may need to both feel safe. I dedicate this book to all twins who live with stories like ours.

To all those who read the story of my young heart recast only slightly through Poppy and Lola and Juniper, then or now, I'm beyond grateful to have been seen and heard.

About the author

Addie Tsai teaches courses in literature, creative writing, dance, and humanities at Houston Community College. She collaborated with Dominic Walsh Dance Theater on *Victor Frankenstein* and *Camille Claudel*, among others. Addie holds an MFA from Warren Wilson College and a PhD in Dance from Texas Woman's University. Her writing has been published in *Banango Street*, *The Offing*, *The Collagist*, *The Feminist Wire*, *Nat. Brut.*, and elsewhere. She is the Nonfiction Editor at *The Grief Diaries* and Senior Associate Editor in Poetry at *The Flexible Persona.*

Also available from Metonymy Press

Little Blue Encyclopedia (for Vivian)
Hazel Jane Plante

nîtisânak
Lindsay Nixon

Lyric Sexology Vol. 1
Trish Salah

Fierce Femmes and Notorious Liars:
A Dangerous Trans Girl's Confabulous Memoir
Kai Cheng Thom

Small Beauty
jiaqing wilson-yang

She Is Sitting in the Night: Re-visioning Thea's Tarot
Oliver Pickle